THE WORDKEEPERS

Coming soon from Duckbill by Jash Sen

Book II and Book III of The Wordkeepers trilogy:
Sky Serpents
Soul Army

THE WORDKEEPERS

Book I of the Trilogy

JASH SEN

duckbill

Duckbill Books

61, Silverline Building, Alapakkam Main Road, Maduravoyal, Chennai 600 095
www.duckbill.in
platypus@duckbill.in

First published by Duckbill Books and westland ltd
Copyright © Jash Sen 2013

10 9 8 7 6 5 4 3 2 1

ISBN 978-93-82618-16-4

Typeset by Ram Das Lal

Printed at Manipal Technologies Limited, Manipal

Also available as an ebook

Children's reading levels vary widely. The general reading levels are
indicated by colour on the back cover. There are three levels: younger
readers, middle readers and young adult readers. Within each level, the
position of the dot indicates the reading complexity. Books for young
adults may contain some slightly mature material.

For my grandfather
Late Professor J.N. Chakraborti

PROLOGUE

Five thousand years ago

The battle was over, but its venom lingered in the air.

In the cold afternoon sun, a group of war-weary men stood in a clump on the dusty battlefield. Bodies were strewn around them, but they seemed immune to the sight and smell of festering corpses.

All their attention was riveted on the two men at the centre. Both were well-built, battle-hardened and in their mid-forties. Their right hands were outstretched in the act of summoning a weapon while the left held their bows at the ready. Even the supreme concentration of summoning could not disguise their utter hatred for each other; it hung like a malevolent shroud over the gathering.

A mediator stood between them, desperation etched on his face, a single jaunty peacock feather standing out in stark contrast to his bloodstained yellow robes and his tense stance. 'Kurukshetra is over and its outcome cannot be altered. Duryodhan is dead, Yudhishthir victorious—there is nothing to be gained by this. Your personal enmity is putting thousands of other lives in jeopardy. Do you realise the consequence of summoning the Brahmashir weapons?'

Neither man moved a muscle, their eyes locked into each other.

'Arjun, Ashwatthama, recall the weapons while there is still time. If you release them, there will be nothing left to rule—no Hastinapur, no Indraprastha, no subjects, no progeny—just a barren landscape where there was once a thriving kingdom. Is this what you fought for? Yours was a righteous war, fought so far for loyalty and obligation. Why sully it with vendetta now?'

With a sigh, as if it caused him great pain, the man on the left lowered his right hand and closed his eyes momentarily, chanting under his breath. Arjun had come to his senses, it seemed. The group relaxed somewhat.

A split second later, a flash rent the air in two and Ashwatthama's right hand held a glowing arrow. He calmly straddled it on his bow, the large blue gem on his forehead glinting in the setting sun.

Krishna spoke in a hurry, 'Ashwatthama, this weapon will let loose the apocalypse if you use it. Redirect it.'

The assembled company gasped in horror. It was

already too late. Everyone knew that Ashwatthama did not have the ability to recall the Brahmashir. Any one of the Brahmashir weapons could destroy their kingdom, and this one would have to be released somewhere or it would combust on the spot, taking everyone with it.

Krishna's voice rang out again, speaking fast, with clear instructions:

'Ashwatthama! There is very little time, so listen carefully. You have to think of a target to which you can direct the Brahmashir. To the northeast of where you are standing, there is a crop field about five hundred yards away. If you direct your weapon there, no lives will be lost, although the ground will stay barren for a generation. But that is the only safe way out for all of us. Do not delay; do it now before the weapon self-combusts.'

For the first time in all this while, Ashwatthama's face betrayed an emotion: a bitter, twisted smile glided across it as he closed his eyes. Every person present turned his eyes in the direction of the crop field, waiting for the telltale mushroom-shaped cloud. Nothing. Just silence.

Then a wail crashed upon their ears—swelling up as more voices joined in. The dreaded cloud had appeared, but over a tent in the Pandav camp. An old woman ran out, dishevelled, mad with grief, flinging herself at Arjun as she wept. Arjun felt himself go cold with foreboding. He knew whose tent it was.

'Lost, lost—the last lamp of Hastinapur, Uttara's son, your grandson—snuffed out even before he lived! The price of fratricide, and you deserve it, all of you! This is truly the end. The Kurus are a dead lot from this day on. Why, oh why did you fight this cursed war?'

She was still ranting and sobbing but Arjun heard no more. The blood pounding in his ears, he leapt at Ashwatthama's throat with his naked sword.

Someone else had got there first.

Quivering with rage, Krishna wrenched the gem from Ashwatthama's forehead, his voice ringing out with terrifying resonance:

'Ashwatthama, for this deliberate, premeditated act of spite, I curse you: you will roam the earth till the end of time, a leper, shunned by all, with a permanently festering wound on your forehead, in continuous pain till the end of the earth. You will know no shelter, no peace, no friends—you will weep for death but it will not arrive.'

On the handsome warrior's forehead there was now a bleeding wound the size of a gold coin. Red, sore blotches were appearing rapidly on his alabaster skin.

Apocalypse had been averted. It had vent all its fury on one man.

PART ONE

Notes from an Immortal

I, Vibhishan, past Lord of the Sinhala land of Lanka, immortal by the grace of my Lord Ram, and the general of the wordkeepers, write the following.

I had to meet her in spite of the circumstances. I was worried. We had suffered losses in the past five years that I, as a general, should be ashamed of. Rasool Elahi was first, ambushed by two demons stuck together like Siamese twins. They couldn't kill him, of course, but they seriously weakened us by taking his amulet. Then a year later, it was my kin, the Sinhalese agent. He held out until his wife was killed in front of him, and he had to surrender the amulet to save his and his daughter's lives. It was more important to live to fight another day. Then the wordkeeper from Bangalore didn't respond, so I had to take some action. We were being systematically hunted down by our opponents. Something was wrong.

Before I could act, the enemy struck a body blow. The wordkeeper was taken; abducted right under my nose. That left my final hope, the new wordkeeper.

So I waited and watched, trying to intercept this child—provided she wished to accept the challenge thrown at her. I had known her clan right from the beginning and had worked closely with them, from her great-great-grandmother onwards. Brave women, all of them. By rights, this girl should be a brave one as well, although at first glimpse, I have to admit I was sorely disappointed. I was thinking of approaching her and gradually introducing myself, but alas! Yet again, I proved to be unworthy of the responsibility my lord had placed on my shoulders.

ANYA

Anya realised with a start that she missed her mother, and was thoroughly surprised.

Anya's parents were both busy professionals with crazy travel schedules. Not that she was complaining. What with her school, her tutor, bharatnatyam classes and martial arts lessons, Anya was a very busy person in her own right. She largely preferred to leave them alone and to be left alone, thank you very much, not that anyone ever asked her for her opinion on the matter.

Even so, she, Daddy and Ma made it a point to be home together for the weekends. It didn't feel right that Ma was away at a conference and not at home, this Sunday. She had left the previous day.

'Did Ma call?' she asked her father casually, careful to keep her voice light. She and her father were sitting at the dining table for breakfast, tucking into steaming hot idlis and coconut chutney.

'She reached her hotel last night, sweetheart;

have some more idlis,' said her father, barely looking up from the Sunday papers. Another half a dozen unread newspapers lay neatly stacked to his right. Why anyone would want to read newspapers, when there were tablets and TV, Anya couldn't understand. It was 2028, after all, not the twentieth century.

But Daddy was like that. He worked hard all week and was supremely lazy on a Sunday, when he read newspaper after newspaper—both national and from across the world. If aliens attacked the earth on a Sunday he'd probably not know until the following morning. He was married to the Sunday papers, in her mother's opinion.

Anya stretched like a cat, her stomach full after the heavy breakfast, before stopping short with a frown. Sunday was also Miss Murthy's day, shit! Miss Murthy was one of those boring tutors people should legally be allowed to strangle. Her voice squeaked. So did her flat shoes. She taught with no imagination whatsoever, but by sticking to exam questions like a leech, she managed to get good grades out of her wards. Two hours of torture every Sunday with Miss Murthy ensured that Anya had both good grades and the right level of cynicism about the education system, a life skill in itself. She excused herself, got up from the breakfast table and headed to the shower adjacent to her bedroom. The sooner she got it over with, the better.

It was then that she noticed the necklace. It was lying behind her shampoo bottle on the bathroom shelf. Her mother wore very little jewellery as a rule, but for as long as she could remember, Anya had seen her wear this necklace and her wedding band. She had once asked if it was an astrological thing, fearing a long lecture from her mother who was a dyed-in-the-wool sceptic. It looked like one—rather functional and a bit crude. But Ma had just laughed and said that it had belonged to her mother, and her grandmother before that. And that Anya would have it one day. An heirloom.

It was a simple necklace, a chain of small silver balls with a pendant hanging from it. The pendant was made of silver and had an old-fashioned ridged pattern on the side. It was oval, like the wickedly gleaming dark red stone inside it. The stone always grabbed Anya's attention. She fancied she could see other colours swirling in its depths. Today it looked maroon.

Why was it here? Ma never even took it off, let alone forgot it. She picked it up and put it away in her secret hiding place in the bathroom, the jar of washing powder. The necklace disappeared in the tiny white grains. Chop, chop, Anya—shower first—she told herself. Otherwise you'll need a couple of toothpicks to prop up your eyelids when Miss Morphine arrives.

Her tutor looked at Anya's answer sheet and sighed. The opaque green, expressionless eyes looked at Anya, who stared back mutinously.

'Just write the answer in the textbook, child,' she cajoled. 'Why do you want to write so much more when both answers will give you an A?'

'I have a name,' muttered Anya under her breath.

'Pardon, dear?'

'I wrote those extra facts because I happen to find them relevant. I've given two extra examples of Akbar's liberal policies which are not even mentioned in the textbook.' Anya didn't bother to reiterate her earlier point.

'The Board-approved research texts are *Medieval India: A Guide* by Dr Rubina Singh and *Akbar: Flawed Genius* by Claudius Doyle, and don't roll your eyes at me, dear,' continued Miss Murthy, unperturbed. 'No other research will be considered for marks,' she added crisply.

Anya stifled a snort and looked out of the window. Her two hours were nearly up. Why rock the boat? She nodded.

For the next twenty minutes, while Miss Murthy read an extract in an unbelievably boring monotone, Anya's mind drifted as she sat and watched her tutor. Although dressed in a silk sari, Miss Murthy had a European complexion, just a shade more yellow than pink. Green eyes peered through thick-rimmed, almost opaque, high-powered glasses. Sandy hair, not blonde, but not the typical Indian dark brown or black either. Anya labelled her tutor's colouring as 'Caucasian; almost.'

'Miss Murthy,' she blurted out. 'Can I ask you something?'

'Hem?' Miss Murthy cleared her throat and blinked. She was not used to being interrupted while reading out loud. She stared blankly at Anya for some time, and then said eventually, 'Ask away, dear.'

'You don't look typically Indian—you know, brown skin, dark hair, dark eyes—are you half something else?' Anya was not happy with how nosy she sounded, but she plodded on nonetheless. Life's too short.

Miss Murthy turned a strange shade, half pink, half yellow—Anya thought she was going to throw up, until she realised that her tutor was blushing! She stammered shyly, fluttering her sandy eyelashes, 'Well, em, I'm half Irish; my late mother was Irish.

That's how I'm so fair.'

Anya smiled her thank you. Vanity, she reflected, was a wonderful thing. For the next ten minutes, Miss Murthy didn't ask her a single question and Anya let her mind drift blissfully, not listening to a word that was being said.

The best part about Sundays were the afternoons. Anya loved the freedom of hanging around, doing nothing. Today she was swinging on her bungalow gate.

The city of Bangalore was dusty, and filled with skyscrapers and sprawling apartment complexes. It had succumbed to the postcolonial pressure of being reborn as Bengaluru, but Anya loved the old name and refused to use the new one. Old-timers in the city—people her parents' age or older—would sigh and look meaningfully at each other when they talked of the old Bangalore, the garden city with its quaint bungalows, where the climate was pleasant throughout the year and so were people's manners. Then they sighed and talked about concrete jungles and the water mafia and the lines in front of posh complexes, where residents queued up with buckets.

Anya didn't mind. She loved this vibrant new city and her life here, warts and all, and didn't particularly care about times gone by.

She and her parents lived in one such posh

complex full of bungalows with garages and gardens and all the mod cons possible, which were considerable, if you were willing to pay. *They* didn't have any water problems, thank goodness. Anya quite enjoyed being rich. A flat is pleasant in its own way—she'd been to a few of her friends' flats—but this was just so much better.

She pushed hard with her left foot, making sure this last swing was a really good one, and braked with the right foot once she'd reached the second gate. Having secured the latch, Anya looked around with a happy sigh. What next? The huge expanse of the garden beckoned and she walked towards it, trying out a little tune unsuccessfully. Anya was a terrible singer, hence her parents' focus on bharatnatyam and taekwondo. She walked in her loose-limbed, athletic way towards the garden. Anya had her father's walk and her mother's complexion.

The garden was her mother's special project. Ma had green fingers. Unlike most self-proclaimed gardeners, she hoed, weeded and pruned her own plants, and they thrived under her care. Every Sunday afternoon, she was to be found in the garden, humming away, talking to her plants. Their garden wasn't one of those ultra-manicured ones with impeccable lawns, but something out of a fairy tale. It was a beautifully undulating space with large trees and almost felt like a wood if you were in the middle.

Anya continued to hum tunelessly as she picked her way through the mulched path at the perimeter; and tripped over something.

She frowned and stopped in her tracks. Yet another rich neighbour who didn't think twice before littering. Her mother always told her she was overreacting when she ranted about people throwing plastic bags in their garden. But honestly, what's the point of living in a fancy place if you don't even have the sense to keep it clean? Clucking with annoyance, she bent down and picked up the offending item.

It was a cheap blue plastic bag, one among countless others strewn across the entire country. This one was recyclable. Wait, there was something solid inside. Anya put her hand in and pulled out a standard-sized glass medicine bottle, the kind that holds multivitamin capsules. It had probably been used to weigh the bag down, so it would land in the right place instead of floating in the air. But why throw an empty bag, and why take so much trouble to make sure it landed just here? Anya gave the bag a good shake to see if anything else came out. Zip. Just bin it, she thought.

Hang on. What were those black marks? Someone had scribbled inside the bag. She turned it inside out, half expecting a rude message, some idiot's idea of a practical joke. She frowned as she read aloud:

Anya, I am taken. Open my red locket and follow the code. Trust no one. Not even Daddy or me.—Ma.

Bullshit.

Did people really think she would fall for that? All I have to do is call Ma, you stupid jerks, she thought. She made a rude gesture in the air with the hand that held the medicine bottle. It rattled. There was something inside. Something glinted in the sunlight. She put in her forefinger and thumb and pulled out a wedding band. It was gold, with an engraving on the inside which said: *Tanya.*

Anya's heart leaped to her mouth at the sight of the familiar object. She had played with her mother's wedding band a million times.

TRUST NO ONE

Rushing straight to her bathroom, Anya shoved her hand into the jar of washing powder and fished out the necklace, unaware that she was holding her breath, until she let it out in one big whoosh when the metal chain glinted dully on her palm. Then she bolted her door and sat down on her bed to think.

She didn't know what to think. What on earth did Ma mean, 'not even Daddy or me'? A peculiar statement. The obvious thing to do was to call her on her mobile and tell her about this silly message. The words 'trust no one' kept hammering in her head; 'trust NO one'. Well, she'd call Ma just the same, just to make sure everything was all right, and she wouldn't mention the note. She made up her mind and took out her mobile from her pocket.

'Shall I connect you?' asked a suave voice.

'Yes.'

'Your most popular contacts are Rohan, Sharmili,

Adil, Ma and NetY Gaming. Do you wish me to connect you to any of these contacts?'

'Ma, Ma, just hurry up!'

'Connecting to Ma,' said the voice, unperturbed and unemotional.

'Yes, Anya, what is it? Quick, I'm in the middle of something,' said her mother's voice at the other end, reassuringly normal and busy.

'Just missing you, Mum ... uh ... just wanted to hear your voice.'

'Oh, sweetheart! Don't you worry, I'll be back on Wednesday.'

'You've not forgotten anything, have you Ma?'

'What do you mean? Forgotten what?'

A sixth sense warned Anya to keep quiet. Trust no one.

'Nothing. Its just that you usually call saying you've left something or the other behind.'

Her mother's voice laughed at the other end, reassuring. 'You know what I think? I think you really missed me and thought up an excuse to call. Now, be nice to Daddy while I'm away. Many hugs. Love you.'

Click.

'Call disconnected,' said the suave voice.

Anya took a deep breath to calm herself. Well, that *sounded* all right. Although it wasn't like Ma to lose something as precious as a wedding ring and not mention it to her. Neither did she talk about the necklace. She should have missed it by now. It didn't add up somehow. Ah well, perhaps people just started their dementia earlier these days, what with the insane work pressure and all. She never did understand how grown-ups' minds worked anyway. Maybe she should mention the amulet to Daddy— just mention it and see what he said.

In significantly better spirits, she trooped down the stairs to the living room, where her father was watching the Sunday Sports Round-up. She was determined not to worry for a while. Daddy was slumped on the sofa with a can of beer in his hand, watching the show with rapt attention. He loved his Sunday afternoon beer and TV. He used to be a sportsperson, but was now reduced to enjoying it vicariously on the screen. Giant three-dimensional images of cars were being projected on the wall opposite, the noise of their screeching tires reaching a deafening crescendo from time to time. Anya could smell the burning rubber. She wrinkled her nose and wished her father would turn down the smell. She sat down next to him, desperately wanting a cuddle but feeling awkward to ask. Some things are just so much easier when you're a kid. Look at diapers.

'Hullo sweetie,' said her father absently, with that glazed look in his eyes that people get when they watch too much television. 'Tennis is up next.' Anya got up to grab a lemon drink from the fridge and settled down next to him, sitting cross-legged, her preferred posture. A glamorous anchor summed up the last segment, which was on racing and after a commercial break, the tennis segment started. The anchor returned and talked about Leonardo Vidal's Grand Slam, the biggest news in tennis for a while.

'Daddy, I want to ask you something,' she began.

Her father nodded, eyes still glued on the screen. 'A very talented player, very talented indeed. It was a pleasure to watch him in the final against Mankovic last week,' he said.

Anya stilled every muscle in her body.

She stared hard at the screen, for something serious had just happened.

Daddy hated Vidal's guts. He was an out-and-out Mankovic fan. Seriously, he was a bit strange about his tennis. He had spent most of last Sunday swearing loudly at the screen. Anya remembered perfectly, because she had to come downstairs and ask him to keep the noise down, a rare moral victory for her. It was almost as bizarre as a person waking up with amnesia and saying, 'Who am I?' More so, for Daddy was clearly in his senses otherwise. A horrible thought flashed through her mind. No, it couldn't be, that's impossible, she told herself firmly.

It was a strange, compelling desire to know the truth that prompted her next move. Forcing her actions to remain normal, she playfully took her father's left hand in her own as she pretended to play with his fingers. It was Daddy's hand all right. The same texture of skin, same sort of podgy fingers, same ring. The tennis set was at 40-40. Good. Looking straight at the screen, she casually pulled out her father's wedding band and tried it on her fingers, one by one. As always, it was a little bigger than her thumb. Her father smiled indulgently and ruffled her hair. She smiled back and put the ring back on his finger.

She had seen what she had needed to. The inside surface of the wedding band spelt her father's name: *Anuj.* All was well. She sighed a big sigh and allowed herself another lemonade. She would talk to Daddy about the amulet. He would have a proper explanation.

She looked at herself in the mirrored bar counter next to the fridge and preened a bit. She never did like her nose. Pushing it up with her middle finger, she checked the final effect. Better. Much better. Should she colour her hair? It was not allowed in school, she knew—but just one red lock in front?

She could easily hide it. Her eyes moved over her reflection, appraising the girl opposite.

Something was not quite right. Why was she alone in the room? The TV was on. She turned round. Daddy was right there, watching TV. Her spine was suddenly a trickle of cold water. Very carefully, she pretended to hunt for the bottle opener, her eyes on the mirror. Still nothing. No other person, not even a shadow of one.

Humans have reflections; they show up in mirrors, they cast shadows. They have to. Her mind raced. What was that *thing* pretending to be her father? Trust no one, trust *no* one, a manic voice in her head hummed.

A HIDDEN MESSAGE

Dinner was a subdued affair. Anya was on edge, and silently finished her food, impatient to go back to her room, where she could think. What kind of creature had no reflection and cast no shadow? If *he* was here, where was her father? Was her mother's voice fake too? Where *were* they? If he meant Anya harm, why hadn't he done anything yet? She looked up surreptitiously, to find her father looking straight at her.

'Something the matter, Anya?' he asked pleasantly enough, but his eyes were watchful. Anya shook her head. Her father talked of this and that, sticking to strictly neutral topics. Anya noticed that he didn't ask her any personal questions. Does he suspect anything? Anya wondered, but his face looked absolutely normal.

She excused herself from the table and sped up the stairs. She showered, brushed her teeth, changed into her nightclothes, switched off her lights and got into bed, asleep as far as the world was concerned. She left her bedroom door half open so she could tell when the thing pretending to be her father went to bed. The locket was clutched tightly in her hand. Once the lights in the rest of the house were off, she would examine it at leisure. She put the necklace away carefully, inside her pillow cover.

The wait seemed like an eternity. At last, she heard her father climb upstairs and saw his familiar podgy shape near her door. He paused; what was he looking at? With a start, Anya realised that her father was slowly opening her bedroom door wider and looking inside. She pretended to shut her eyes and breathed the deep, regular breathing of a person asleep. Then, a small slip. Through half-closed eyes, Anya watched in silent horror as her father's familiar shape went from podgy to lean on the deserted stairwell. The impostor had assumed it was safe to assume his real shape. People always underestimate children, thought Anya. She held her breath until she heard her parents' bedroom door shut.

Another twenty minutes.

In the silent house, she could hear the click of the switch of the lamp in her parents' room as it was turned off.

Anya waited for a while before she pulled out the necklace for a closer inspection. Moonlight was streaming in through the window. The locket gleamed purple in the semi-darkness. Anya felt for a catch or a little lever—how does one open a locket? The outside bit was smooth and metallic. It didn't look like it could be opened that way. She felt the locket with her fingers, trying to detect a ridge, a bump, an unevenness.

There. Just under the metal loop through which the chain passed, a slight bump under her thumb, like the head of a small pin. Holding her breath in excitement, she pressed it. Nothing happened at first. After she had kept the pressure on for about five seconds, a red light started coming out of the stone, as it swung out on the tiniest hinge.

On the inner side of the stone was inscribed the image of a man on a winged horse. And inside the locket was a tiny piece of paper. It said: BOIOIBOB.

Anya lay under her thin sheet in the dark, her mind working at breakneck speed. So the necklace meant something after all. She had always wished it would, for she was fond of treasure hunts and whodunits. But how could she figure out what the hidden message in the necklace was? Who was the person in the engraving? Anya had never seen a Hindu god with a winged horse before, although she knew of the Greek legend of Perseus and Pegasus. This image was very different. The man was in traditional Indian clothing—a salwar, turban, sandals, armour. It was like any other mythological portrait, a very stylised image, with little resemblance to real people of today. Not much to go upon.

Anya pressed her mobile to activate the bluish light. Now for the piece of paper. What could BOIOIBOB signify? An acronym in English? The first letter of each word in a coded message? She pronounced Boioibob in her head, but that was just gibberish. Possible acronyms for the letters spawned 'Boobi Bio', which made her giggle, but was otherwise unhelpful.

The little giggle threatened to turn hysterical, so she pinched herself hard. It helped her vent some of the stress she had been feeling all day. She yawned silently, opening her mouth wide like a cat's. It had been a long day and there was school tomorrow. Better get some shut-eye, Anya. Her eyes closed, lids weighed down by sleep. She couldn't shake off the uneasy feeling, though—as if she was under surveillance.

Had she looked out the window, she would have realised why.

Anya was dreaming.

She was dreaming of a holiday with her mother,

in hills clad with giant deodar trees. Ma was holding her hand and showing her something in the sky. Anya looked up at the sky and caught a glimpse of a giant bird, before the dream changed to a black vacuum. She knew she was still dreaming, but a parallel track in her mind was playing out a movie that she felt compelled to watch. It seemed terribly important to see the whole dream and to remember it.

A man filled her entire vision. A gigantic man, well-built, clad in a dhoti and a hand-sewn kurta. Both had been some other colour originally, but the fabric had turned a muddy brown with dirt and extreme age. The giant walked slowly, as if in pain. Anya found she was gaining on him in spite of his large strides. She stopped in her tracks as she came closer to him. Every inch of exposed skin was covered with oozing sores, pus and blood. They seeped through his bandages.

Anya shuddered involuntarily and the giant seemed to sense her presence. He turned around to face her. Lank, grey, shoulder-length hair covered his face, so Anya could see very little of his expression. She mustered up all her courage and walked up to the man.

'Who are you?' she demanded, pretending to a bravery she did not feel. 'What do you want?'

In response, the man brushed the grey strands away from his face and turned towards her. Right where his hair was parted at the forehead, was a gaping black hole. It was as large as her fist. Dried blood had crusted around it, but it still continued to ooze a slow trickle of pus and blood.

The man's blackened teeth came into view as he opened his mouth to speak. 'When, wordkeeper, when? How long must I wait for my redeemer?' He reached out a festering arm and shook her by the shoulder.

Anya screamed in her dream, but slept on.

Unknown to her, a giant eye, an eye as tall as her window, with a green iris and sandy lashes, kept a steady watch on her throughout the night.

ESCAPE!

Morning was horrible. Anya's head throbbed in an angry rhythm as she rubbed balm on her forehead. Ditching school was an option; she needed time to think and to look through her mother's stuff for clues. Fortunately, she was saved the trouble of a lengthy explanation to the stranger posing as her father as her headache was a very real one. It also served as an excellent excuse for silence at the breakfast table.

When he asked her what was wrong, she quite truthfully told him that she had had a nightmare and the splitting headache was a consequence of that. He himself decided that she needed a day's rest and called up the school. Once he finally waved goodbye and got into the car, Anya sighed in relief. She was alone at last, to think and to search the house for clues if necessary.

She took a quick shower and put on the necklace, taking care to button up her shirt so it wouldn't show. Then she went to her room and tidied it up. Not her favourite pastime, granted, but if she didn't want anyone going through her things it was the safest option.

After that she went into her mother's study, taking care to check that the help were all downstairs. She switched on her PC, a slim sliver of steel, and logged on to her mail. If anyone looked in, she was doing what teenagers normally do when they're on they're own—surfing the net. Being a genuine flesh-and-blood teenager, that's exactly what she did for the next ten minutes, telling herself it was needed to allay any suspicions.

Finally, with a satisfied sigh, she logged off and looked around her mother's desk. Mostly files, keys, cheque books and the like. Sighing, Anya picked up the top one, titled 'Anuj Sharma'. She noticed that they were alphabetically organised from 'Anuj Sharma' to 'Visas'. A long, long day, Anya, she told herself, resigning herself to some serious, tedious searching.

The top file yielded nothing interesting. As she looked through the second file, labelled with her name, some interesting facts came to light. Her joint account with her mother had quite a bit of money, for one thing. The latest balance showed Rs 15,00,000. A handwritten note by her mother also said that Anya had fifty gold coins of ten grams each in their shared bank locker. Good. All she had to do was to use the ATM card to withdraw cash and take things out of the locker.

She started scrutinising the list of things in the bank locker and froze. At the top, it said: Bank of Baroda Vault No. B-0101.

BOIOIBOB! So that was it! The secret code was the number to her own bank vault. Whatever was to be found next, would be there.

Anya swiftly put the files back in their place, taking care to remove the vault list and the vault key first. Things must look undisturbed. The files are usually the first thing anyone would go through: look at me, she thought. Luckily for her, she had her own ATM card. Her mother had always encouraged Anya to understand personal finance. Was this why? Had Ma always expected that something like this would happen?

She lay on her bed and went over the events of the past two days, seeing each one as a small video clip in her brain. She had last seen her mother when she kissed her goodbye two days ago. Anya was sure her mother had checked her reflection in the hall mirror. Had she also cast a shadow? She wasn't certain. Her mother had waited outside for the airport cab, not wanting to be late.

What had made her take out the multivitamin bottle from her bag, toss her ring into it and scrawl a message into a plastic bag, before tossing the whole package inside the garden as a warning? What had she seen? Why couldn't she escape? And most importantly, where was she now?

And what about her father? Had the impostor taken his place before or after her mother had left? Somehow, she felt the answer lay with Ma. She was the one who'd left clues and tried to warn Anya.

Anya looked up at the ceiling and evaluated her options. It was up to her to rescue her mother. Ma would tell her what to do next; she would know how to find Daddy. She could rescue Ma only when she knew where to go. But keeping the pendant and the information in the vault with herself was even more critical. Her mother had clearly planned for this eventuality. There was just one thing left to find out: she was a minor; could she get in and operate their bank locker without her mother? How?

Fifteen more minutes of dogged thinking and she had a plan. Well, it was at least worth a shot. Anya sat at her PC again and typed out a note:

Dear Lakshmi,

I'm laid low with a nasty bout of flu after my last tour. There's a wedding we have to go to tonight. Since Anya's my joint account holder, she'll go in and get out a piece of jewellery for me. I know she's still a minor, but I was hoping you'd let her in, especially since you've seen us together for the past four years. It would be a huge favour.

How's everything else otherwise?

Best regards,

Tanya

She surveyed her efforts. Satisfied, she printed out the document, and after a few attempts, turned out a decent forgery of her mother's signature, mentally congratulating herself for having done it a fair number of times on detention slips. One never knows what turns out to be of use in this life. She grinned impishly to herself, and then carefully pressed the backspace key, until Document 1 was blank again. She quit the word processor, declining to save. There! Trace that if you can!

Anya dressed carefully for the bank. She didn't want to look like she was going somewhere important, or was carrying anything of value, but she also wanted to be taken seriously once she got there. In the end, she decided on her school bag, jeans and a smart(ish) t-shirt. On her way out, she shouted to no one in particular, 'I'm off to the library!' Her housekeeper would lock the door behind her and wait at least until lunchtime before she got alarmed and called anyone. Which gave her a few hours to get ahead. The large mirror in the hall had been removed, she noticed.

To her surprise, a complete stranger came up to the door. This man looked more like a secret-service agent than anything else; he even wore the regulation grey suit and gold-framed Ray-Ban Aviators.

'Dashrath isn't here today, miss—I'm his temporary replacement. My name is Francis. Are you going out? Would you like me to drop you anywhere in the car?'

'What happened to the mirror here?'

'Taken for cleaning, miss. It's part of routine maintenance.'

Anya shrugged. Look casual. Your life might depend on it. 'I don't need a lift, thanks. My headache's better, so I'm just heading to the club library, and then maybe for a little walk. I just couldn't manage to work on the home comp, and I think I need to clear my head for my project submission tomorrow.' Anya was a smooth liar.

'When will you be back, miss, in case sir calls?'

I bet you'll be the one to call him, thought Anya, completely on her guard now.

'An hour at the most,' she replied, with a carefree smile. 'Look Francis, I'm carrying my mobile, just call if you need me, okay?'

She turned away, and kept her walk jaunty until she was out of his line of vision, then broke into a run. She ran until she found a taxi to take her to the branch on Magyar Road.

Shutting the door, Francis dialled a number and had a whispered conversation for a minute. Then he nodded and disconnected the phone, which briefly flashed 'Anuj Sharma Cell' before the light died out. He asked for a second number and had a brief talk.

Absentmindedly taking off his Ray-Bans, he wiped them with a handkerchief while he thought of something else. His eyes were green, with sandy lashes.

Cecilia Murthy sat at the dressing table of her shabby one-bedroom flat in Domlur. She was still wearing a Kanjivaram sari and rubber slippers; there was nonetheless something different about her appearance. Her left eyelid was tightly shut, sunk into its socket. Her eye lay on the dressing table, covered with a fine layer of talcum powder, its green pupil swivelling all over the white sphere. It finally stopped, resting on her face. Cecilia finished putting on her lipstick, and much in the manner of wearing a contact lens, picked up the eye, wiped it clean with her pallu and inserted it into her left eye socket. Blinking her sandy lashes a couple of times, she checked the end result. Fine, as always.

Her phone rang, its silky male voice announcing, 'Francis.' She picked it up and listened intently, deactivating the default speakerphone. Her body language changed; she was suddenly alert, like a hunter on a trail.

'Where is she now?' was all she said.

Putting her phone away, she shook her head in irritation. Francis was getting careless. She had told him the child was a sharp one. She had taught the kid for three years, after all. It wasn't a big deal tracking her down, just an extra job that could have been avoided. The day was hot; she would rather have rested indoors. What a waste, after having kept an eye on her all night. It was now imperative to know where she was headed. Cecilia mulled over the options.

The girl would need money. She logged on to the Sharmas' bank accounts, checking for transactions. There were none. There was no money in the house, she knew. Francis had checked. That left the unusual option of physical cash, stashed away somewhere. A vault, perhaps? A logical first step, anyway. She typed in a few details and five bank branches popped up. Cecilia chose to start with the nearest one—Magyar Road.

Anya walked into the branch and smiled broadly at the security guard, whom she had known since the first day she had come there, four years ago. He smiled back at her just as broadly from behind his enormous moustache.

'Ah, Anya baby, on your own today, I see. Where's your mother?'

'Fever,' smiled Anya. 'I have to give this letter to Lakshmi Aunty.' She waved the envelope at him.

He motioned her inside, not bothering to check her with the metal detector. She walked up to the vault manager, smiling what she hoped was a shy, disarming smile.

'Look who's here,' said the plump lady behind the desk, offering Anya a bowl of candy. Anya took a moment to marvel at the ancient computer on her desk with its flat-screen monitor. Clearly the government considered projections a bit too revolutionary. It should be a qualified antique, she thought.

'Try the melon ones, they're a new flavour,' the lady suggested, bringing her back to the present. 'So, what can I do for you today, Anya?'

'Lakshmi Aunty, Ma's got the flu, so she asked me to give you this,' said Anya, giving her the letter and helping herself to the melon drops. It was crucial to act casual, even if she was fervently praying that the woman sitting opposite wouldn't decide to call her mother and be solicitous.

The manager read the letter carefully and looked at her; a strange watery sparkle in her eyes, as if she was sorry for her. Then she said in her usual pleasant, businesslike manner, 'I'm sure we can allow you to operate the vault. Come with me.'

She rose noisily from her leather chair, picked up a heavy bunch of keys and set off towards the vault. Anya followed her, not believing her luck.

'Did you know your mother and I were at school together?' Lakshmi Aunty asked suddenly. Anya shook her head, surprised. She had assumed that her mother had got to know Lakshmi Aunty only since she'd started coming to this bank.

The vault gate creaked as Lakshmi Aunty pushed it open. Stepping inside, she beckoned Anya in. Vault B-0101 was the lowest one at the back. Anya and the manager kneeled and turned the keys simultaneously. The little door clicked and swung open. Smiling at

Anya, the manager left the room, shutting the door behind her.

Anya took a deep breath and put her hand inside the vault. Mysterious bundles wrapped in plastic popped out. She felt for any last bits that might be left behind, and her hand closed on an envelope. Pulling it out, she saw that it was a plain white one, with her mother's handwriting proclaiming in clear block letters: ANYA—READ THIS FIRST.

Anya opened the envelope. A card fell out. It said:

Take the gold coins and the cash. There are fifteen hundred notes of a thousand rupees each. Do not use the ATM card from now on. All technology can be tracked, so get off the grid. Use pens, paper, cash, the post.

Go to Asirgarh Fort at Burhanpur. You will be met there. Leave immediately. Read the rest on your way.

Her mobile vibrated, startling her. The voice announced in a soft whisper: 'Daddy mobile'. Anya stared at the phone, transfixed. She quickly stuffed everything in her bag, thanked the manager and stepped outside in the sun.

After a moment's hesitation, she hailed a taxi and asked it to take her to City Station. The taxi weaved its way through the busy street like a drunken ladybird. Her mobile was vibrating furiously again.

'Home', said the voice this time. She ignored it and tried to calm herself. Switching off the phone, she stuffed it under the seat of the taxi.

At fourteen, her life had suddenly turned upside down.

Had she been a little less preoccupied, she would have noticed Miss Murthy running surprisingly fast on the left pavement and talking into her mobile.

Francis received his instructions on his phone. He was to stay put at the house to guard against any potential intruders. While it was curious that the girl was stepping out, it was not yet critical to monitor her every move. There was no way she could know anything was amiss. The shapeshifters were doing a stellar job. Another agent would be sent to shadow the girl if necessary. Things were going as planned. It was more of a precaution, if anything.

Francis was an experienced agent who knew the importance of following orders. There was no point in playing the hero in a sensitive situation like this. Back-up would be sent shortly, anyway.

Yet, something didn't add up. The extra brightness in the girl's eyes, the forced casual air; years of experience told him that she was hiding something. There was something about that girl.

It was more to soothe his own sixth sense than for any real reason that he decided to search the girl's room. He tiptoed up the stairs in his rubber-soled shoes and pushed Anya's bedroom door open. A quick check told him that she hadn't packed any clothes. Good. She's probably not staying away then. For all he knew, she could be bunking school to catch a movie or meet a boyfriend—typical fourteen-year-old clandestine stuff. He shrugged his shoulders and turned the doorknob.

That was when something caught his eye. Something blue, stuffed hastily under the mattress, which peeped out just a bit. He turned back, strode up to the bed and pulled out the blue plastic bag. The black lettering was clearly visible from the outside.

The situation changed in a flash. He dialled the last number on his mobile and said in his crisp voice: 'She knows. And she's got it.'

Anya walked up to the ticket counter and weighed her options. As far as she remembered from her sketchy knowledge of India's historical map, Burhanpur was roughly to the north of where she was. It was critical to leave Bangalore and head out somewhere. She looked at the large wooden timetable hanging from the high ceiling, a beautiful colonial relic.

The Karnataka-Kerala express was due to come in and halt for an hour at two-thirty. That was an hour from now. She couldn't risk being in one place for that long. It was imperative that she left the city quickly and discreetly.

'Go to platform two,' said a voice, softly, but quite clearly, close to her ear. Anya spun around, terrified, but could see no one.

'The Nagpur train,' said the voice again.

Who was it, she thought to herself, as she scanned the timetable again. Am I hearing things? Is this is a friend or an enemy?

'Friend,' said the voice.

The express to Nagpur was waiting at platform two. She debated internally for a moment, then walked up to the train and boarded it. She headed to the first-class compartment, shutting the door to the air-conditioned coach behind her. There was no time to buy a ticket. She would deal with that when she had to.

The train was running fairly empty. It wasn't peak season and school holidays had just finished. She put her shoulder bag down beside her and took a window seat.

There was only one other occupant in the coupé, who was wrapped up completely in a blanket and dozing on the seat opposite. All she could see were this person's feet. Anya amused herself for a few seconds staring at them. The second toe on each foot was much longer than the big toe, almost an inch longer. Her co-passenger slept on, oblivious. She gave herself a little shake to bring herself back to the present, rummaged in her bag and took out the letter.

AN EMERGENCY MEETING

The gigantic space pod rested on the barren landscape of the planet. Its five moons were visible, roughly equidistant from each other, in partial shadow at this time of the night. Surrounding the pod were smaller pods, some residential, some administrative, each one bearing the red and black ensign of the city state of Vishasha—a red owl on a black background. Vishasha was a military dictatorship run by the Supremo, assisted by a trusted army of his followers, many of whom were also family members. The most powerful of all its bodies was the Security Council, its secret service unit, run with an iron hand by its leader, General Kokh.

The Security Council had been called for the second time in a week, indicating a state of high emergency. It was routine for the twelve members to meet once in six months. But the warning had come: the Enemy's existence had been proven beyond doubt by the Seer's vision and it was imperative that the threat be neutralised soon, while the Enemy was still unprepared. The task would be exponentially more difficult a decade later.

The Council had two guests with them—their best agents specialising in covert assignments. Both were highly trained eliminators. They spoke all the major human languages, both past and present. And they were both ruthless, with impeccable records when it came to extracting information from those unwilling to part with it. One was male, the other female.

General Kokh was presiding. He was the head of the Security Council and reported only to the Supremo. He was large even by usual Vishasha standards, his powerful hands waving as he spoke, his blind eyes behind dark glasses focusing on no one in particular, yet commanding everyone's attention without effort. Twelve members—men, women and of indeterminate gender—sat ramrod straight, listening with rapt attention. The General's aide-de-camp stood behind him, as still as a sculpture.

'Councillors, before we start, let me introduce you to two of our newest members—the brother and sister crack operative team of Anrit and Nirritti. They have proved exemplary on the field and the Supremo has promoted them to Councillor status as a reward.'

A slim young man and a dark woman with long blonde hair nodded their greetings.

'I will have to fill you two in, of course, so I'll ask the older members to bear with me for a moment.'

'What do we know so far, General?' asked the young man.

'Colonel Anrit, there is a prophecy about these times, one which the Council aims to prevent from happening. This prophecy talks about an Enemy of our state who is going to pose a major threat to the continuation of life as it stands on Earth, our undisturbed utilisation of all its resources, human or otherwise, and consequently, our existence. The broader environment preceding this Enemy's appearance is in place—frequent political and economic upheavals, violence across borders and within them, the lack of a moral compass—the usual stuff of doomsday soothsayers.

'However, there was one specific indicator that we knew of: the Enemy would be born when the Sun, Moon and Jupiter conjunct Pushya Nakshatra in Cancer. This happened on July 26, human year 2014 AD, that is, fourteen human years ago. We are yet to find out the whereabouts of this child. Our orders are to exterminate the Enemy as soon as he or she is found.

The Seer, who foretells all, has sent word about

the existence of the Enemy. She has also claimed that the Enemy is an avatar of Vishnu. It has been the decision of the Supremo, endorsed by myself, to counter the threat as quickly and in as covert a manner as possible. Any delay will allow the Enemy to recruit followers, and our task will be that much more difficult. We don't want any publicity about martyrdom and we do not wish to churn sentiments on Earth, where we are consolidating our presence.'

'We have been on the lookout for more than twenty years now,' said a young, red-haired soldier, raising an eyebrow. 'First to exterminate the possible parents, then the newborn, and now the child. Why this sudden spurt in our activity, General? New developments?'

'Unfortunately, Captain Himsa, the Enemy's existence is a secret closely guarded by an ancient band of protecting clans called the wordkeepers. Originally ten in number, the clans are spread across the globe and are of different nationalities and faiths. They know the prophecy and are also aware of the Enemy's coming, except, as with all weaker races, they think he, or she, is a messiah of sorts, here to rescue them from all their problems.' He paused and smiled a thin smile.

'Therefore, although parts of the prophecy have been disseminated to the public, very little is known in reality about where, when and how the Enemy will emerge. Even the ten clans did not know the information fully, a security measure against betrayal or capture. However, by systematically destroying three of the ten clans, we now have a partial picture of the threat. Any questions?' The General paused, surveying his group in an unseeing stare. His aide held his arm lightly, as usual.

'One more thing: the only way to identify a wordkeeper is through an amulet worn by him or her. It's a silver oval set with a dark red stone, which passes from generation to generation, within the clan. The stones are of great intrinsic value themselves. The Supremo is known to have preferred to obtain the stone amulet even if it meant a wordkeeper's escape, on occasion. Based on the information received from one of our sources on Earth, Cecilia Murthy, we have identified and apprehended the wordkeeper from the fourth clan. Anrit and Nirritti were invaluable in the capture of our fourth wordkeeper—Tanya Sharma, of Bangalore.'

He touched a button on the desk and the wall behind him was transformed into a giant screen. A woman's face, bloody and battered, with one swollen eyelid, looked at them. She was gasping for breath. There were electrodes attached to her head, her fingertips, her toes and crisscrossed across her torso.

She stared at the screen dully, before fainting in a dead heap on the floor. The General's aide-de-camp switched the screen off.

'There's just one problem,' continued the General. 'The amulet is missing. We don't know if she's transferred it to the next appointed wordkeeper or not. Neither Tanya, nor her husband Anuj, who is being held in a separate location, is talking. He has cracked under the pressure, but probably knows nothing. Their daughter has been under our watch for the past twenty-four hours. By right, she should be the next wordkeeper, but she is definitely unaware of the existence of the amulet, or indeed, of her parents being in any danger.'

'General, there is a feed from Earth,' pointed out one of the Council members. 'One of your agents.'

The screen behind General Kokh was flickering. With a flick of the wrist, the General steadied the broadcast.

Francis' face loomed over them. 'I'm afraid I have bad news, General. I have just heard from Agent Murthy that the girl was seen in a taxi heading towards Bangalore City station. Clearly, she is on the run. Agent Murthy could not follow her as she was on foot. The girl told me she was heading out for a while, and looking at her appearance, I thought she would definitely return.'

'No harm done, Agent, it's going as planned,' the General started magnanimously, but was interrupted.

'I respectfully would like to say, sir, that the girl has probably taken the missing amulet with her.'

'Fool! I told you specifically not to underestimate anyone on this mission. Find the train she boarded. And tell Agent Murthy to set the tracker on her. We must have the amulet—it's the Supremo's direct order!' The screen disappeared with a flicker as he waved it away in irritation.

He addressed the Council again, his tone crisp with annoyance.

'I am sure you understand the criticality of the amulets. The Supremo's strict instructions are to deliver them to him personally. Anrit and Nirritti are our choice for the mission. Incidentally, apart from their other considerable skills, Anrit and Nirritti are also shapeshifters.'

The Council applauded by thumping the table in front of them, and all eyes turned towards the agents.

Anuj and Tanya Sharma smiled back at them.

FAMILY REUNION

The Council was relaxing in the smoking room after their sumptuous dinner; most of the diners nursed a goblet of brandy and some had also lit up the odd cigar. All twelve men and women seemed to be in a convivial mood. Looking at them now, it was difficult to imagine that their last topic of discussion had been an assassination plot.

Anrit glanced surreptitiously at the members. The women first. Sergeant Durukti was shrivelled, tall and angular with a frown between her eyebrows. She had barely spoken a word all evening, choosing mostly to observe the proceedings, and nod if she agreed with any of the points made. Durukti was not a warrior, like the rest of the Council. Her powers lay in her bitter and morbid words, always spoken to destroy. Hers were the words that killed. She was called upon to break brave warriors when torture of the physical kind failed. She always succeeded.

At the Security Council, Durukti took notes, as she was a quick scribe. She was also the Supremo's personal secretary, and present at all his meetings.

Himsa was more garrulous. Her shiny red lacquered nails grabbed attention. She was all animal passion, tossing her red mane-like hair back as she laughed her throaty laugh, her eyes appraising Anrit.

Himsa's star was on the rise in Vishasha. She was fearless in battle, a quality much prized by her General. The armies she led fought with an extra ferocity, bringing the Supremo his most stellar victories on Earth. Her eyes seemed hazel until they focussed on something she liked. Liked? No, coveted. Then they turned a tawny yellow and gave her face a manic glow. Whereas Durukti seemed to be decaying, Himsa was terribly alive.

Major Dambha had an outwardly confident air, the kind that a less astute person than Anrit would have been taken in by. A few lank strands of hair were plastered to his forehead. He was one of the Council's most valued researchers, with a talent for ferreting out the truth. Anrit wondered if that was a rumour put out by the Major himself. He spoke with a bluster that Anrit saw through easily as acute nervousness—what do you have to hide, Major? Then again, don't we all have something?

His eyes shifted to Major Bhay's enormous

frame while the latter conversed with Mrityu. He immediately looked away. Now, there was a person that no one wished to cross. Bhay was gigantic, coal black, with scorching yellow eyes. His tiny irises darted maniacally across everyone's face as he spoke, in a constant silent challenge. Anrit noticed that, like him, the others barely met Bhay's gaze. He seemed to intimidate everyone by his very presence.

Except Mrityu, who was calmly engaged in conversation with the demon, his skull-like face, emaciated frame and yellow teeth standing out in stark contrast with the appearance of his companion. Yet, his shrivelled form seemed to command respect, even fear, from all those present. Rumour had it that Mrityu wasn't really one of them. There was an odd dispassionate trait in him and he seemed to look at everyone in the same way, appraisingly, as a potential target to kill, in his cold, unemotional way. Members of the Security Council were no exception. Mrityu was his own master and no one else's. He was in Vishasha because it suited him.

Anrit felt a chill run down his own spine as Mrityu gazed at him in mid-conversation. Why were they all here? Why was Earth so very important to the Supremo? He had a strong presence there anyway. He felt a pair of eyes watching him; Nirritti was weaving through the crowd, walking up to him, still in her human form, like himself.

'The Supremo doesn't want to play second fiddle any more. It's about legitimacy,' she whispered in his ear, guessing the direction of his thoughts.

'I wondered when you'd step up,' he said dryly, on his guard. Nirritti could be unpredictable, especially in the corridors of power. 'So you think he wants centrestage?'

'The Supremo wants to be recognised as the one true lord of humankind, instead of the many existing deities and prophets. This is his age after all. Humans have long put gold and vices above every other priority, just paying lip service to Vishnu all the while. No challenge will be allowed to exist. The Enemy, even if it is a child, is a challenge and needs to be removed from his path.'

'What about those who don't accept him?'

'A miniscule number. Just look at the humans. They all worship the Supremo first. Who on Earth cannot be bought today with gold, or land, or power, or fame? The rest will obviously come to heel or be dealt with.'

Anrit took a drink and sipped gingerly. He didn't like the sound of 'dealt with' much. As a rule, he preferred subterfuge, leaving violence to others.

'What do you think of them after all these years? Quite the family reunion.' Her voice was as cold as ice.

'We've always had more a successful working relationship than anything else,' he responded, careful to keep his voice neutral. 'And anyway, you know that families like ours tend to work and play together. We're a close-knit bunch; with our interests, we have to be.'

The two of them shifted their gaze to the motley group of Council members that remained. They were huddled together, heads bent in conversation, a clique within a clique—Vyadhi, Jara, Shoke, Trishna and Krodhe. Although vastly different in appearance, personality and skills, they nonetheless shared a certain ambivalent, unisexual appeal. Trishna's hoarse voice belied her outward femininity, whereas Vyadhi and Jara sported plucked eyebrows and lacquered nails, in addition to obsessively groomed facial hair. They were all members of the elite Third Gender Task Force, a regiment formed of the best eunuch officers that Vishasha offered.

Nirritti smiled her icy smile. 'Pity our nephews and nieces are so fruitless. Imagine what we could have accomplished if there were a few more generations of the family.'

For Vishasha was a rather inbred world. It was common for brothers and sisters to marry in Vishasha. While this meant wealth and power multiplied, it also meant that mutations and deformities were common. On Vishasha, incest was a way of life.

Leaving the Security Council to their post-dinner drinks, General Kokh moved to his inner sanctum, his aide close behind him. The hesitancy in his steps gradually reduced as he approached the chamber. His aide maintained the light hold, however. The automatic doors slid silently open with the General's muttered command and shut just as noiselessly behind him. His aide released his hold and relaxed his stance as the General strode confidently to his desk and took off the dark glasses.

The chamber consisted of a bed and a large wardrobe with mostly military and a few civilian outfits, a sofa for visitors and a large desk with three chairs: a leather swivel one for the General and two smaller ones opposite it for visitors. It was on one of these that his aide sat down, without asking for permission. Vikokh was General Kokh's twin. Within closed doors, there was a subtle shift in their relationship. Here, Vikokh seemed to exude a greater air of self-assurance.

The General folded his dark glasses and placed them on the desk with the precision of a surgeon: his vision was evidently normal, if not excellent.

In the confines of his high-security disaster-proof and sealed chamber he felt free to let go of the elaborate subterfuge.

'Pointless pretence. The blindness thing. Why keep it going?' asked the General, his voice gruff. He spoke in the staccato style he reserved for more informal situations.

Vikokh threw his jacket on the arm of a sofa, hitched up his trousers, and said, 'You mean, tell them that our true form is that of conjoined twins—invincible when our bodies touch? No thanks, I think we'll keep that to ourselves. Alliances are shifting sands. Let's not divulge critical information based on them.'

'The Supremo's impatient. Feels we're not doing a good enough job. It's been fourteen years—the human should be in our grasp by now. Each passing day is an increased threat to our existence.'

Vikokh was toying with a small flag of Vishasha. He replied crisply, 'Our agents are on the field both on Vishasha and on Earth; the fourth wordkeeper has already fallen; we'll get the rest as well. It would be useful to know the gender, though. Are you sure your information's correct? The Seer has said nothing about it?'

The General grunted. 'A gap-toothed cackle and a date. We're keeping a close watch on the Sindhu river valley. It's highly likely that all of the Indian subcontinent and some of China are fertile grounds for our search. But nothing to stop the Enemy from being anywhere else on Earth, or even in Vishasha itself.'

'A fourteen-year-old moving from Earth to Vishasha? Impossible!'

'You forget, Vikokh, that it was born with powers that are unheard of on Earth and rare even in Vishasha. Never underestimate the Enemy … or the Seer's words,' said the General in a tone that indicated that the discussion was over. 'Get me that bottle of Al Oudh, will you? I have to meet the Supremo now and I feel quite breathless after one of our interviews—a dash of cologne really helps.'

'Get it yourself,' retorted his aide in a shockingly disrespectful voice. He could get away with it.

THE SEER

The Supremo's personal pod was inaccessible to all except his most trusted lieutenants. He usually preferred to meet his team at official venues. General Kokh was one of the few to have the honour of visiting him at his residence.

Tonight, however, the Supremo was his escort to another meeting. The General sat and waited patiently for his buzzer to go off. He didn't have to wait long. A large moon-like asteroid enveloped in mist appeared on his oculus, a screen that showed him what was directly above on the surface, for the General's abode was deep under the ground. General Kokh tapped his brother on the shoulder and both men disappeared through the reinforced metal walls, their arms linked.

They found themselves in a brilliant white hemisphere, the upper half of the pod, the Supremo's public domain. They were seated on a long, white sofa in the softest leather. Behind them was a mahogany twenty-seater table. In front of them was a massive desk of black, polished wood, with gold edgings, flanked by two huge, circular white rugs made of silk. Behind the desk, where the hemisphere nearly ended, was a domed staircase leading down to the sanctum sanctorum, the Supremo's living quarters. The chair behind the desk was made of pure gold. On it was seated an enormous figure. The Supremo.

His snout-like face, under its mane of curly black hair, surveyed them in an unblinking stare. His black uniform with its thick gold braiding dazzled their eyes. As the twins had expected, the room was heavily, even cloyingly scented—but an all-pervading putrid smell, like rotten corpses, filled the air. Years of experience ensured that both men kept their faces impassive, although their complexions paled under the onslaught.

'Greetings Kokh-Vikokh. I trust all's well?' The voice was unexpectedly soft and seductive. A large tongue lolled out, unguarded. The Supremo often had a problem with the size of his tongue. His lieutenants knew better than to ever mention it.

'We are well, Supremo, just surprised at this rare honour,' replied Vikokh, careful with his words.

'Take a look outside,' said the Supremo, not explaining himself yet.

The landscape had changed; they were hovering above Earth, over a barren patch of land with a few flickering fires. Skulls and bones were strewn all over. It was isolated, although the bustle of the city surrounding the spot could be seen below.

'A cremation ground. Where exactly are we?'

'At Kaalikshetra—or Kolkata as it's now called. That is Keoratola, a favourite spot for our quarry,' replied the Supremo. 'I have a guest for you two, I think you'll find her both interesting and informative, especially given the task at hand.' He pressed a buzzer on his desk and spoke into it: 'Bring Dhoomavati up, Durukti.'

'You have the Seer for us, Supremo? Has she anything new to tell?' Vikokh leaned forward, his voice sharpening in excitement. The Seer had not been seen by anyone on Vishasha but Kali, and was a subject of endless speculation.

'You two are masters at ferreting out the truth. Who knows, seeing her in person and discussing the prophecy might bring up some clues. Perhaps there's something I haven't identified yet that you'll find. But I have to warn you, she's in a foul mood—didn't take kindly to being brought here from Earth, I expect. Got a sharp tongue, too, so watch your temper. And remember she's a goddess. You don't want to get blown to smithereens with a curse.'

'No risk of that one while we're together, Supremo,' said General Kokh, touching his brother's arm lightly.

A most ungodly goddess entered the room. Dhoomavati looked like a mad old beggar in the last stages of starvation. She was enveloped in a cloud of smoke, one hand clutching a half-smoked cigarette, the other, a winnowing basket. Her matted hair was white but nicotine-stained. Cigarettes stuck in the tangles made her head look like an albino porcupine. Her dark skin was as wrinkled as crepe paper, either from extreme old age or excessive smoking—it was difficult to say which. Her tattered sari, once white, now muddy, hung loose on her emaciated figure. Her eyes were bloodshot and she seemed drunk.

She stood with her hands on her hips, swaying slightly. The cigarette smouldered near her right hip, burning a hole in her sari, but she didn't seem to notice. She took one last drag and threw it on the plush white carpet, unconcerned.

'Supremo? That's what you're calling yourself these days? Whatever happened to the good, old-fashioned name your father gave you, eh, Kali?' She paused and allowed herself a look round the room. 'Nice pad you've got yourself—not bad for a banished god, not bad at all! A far cry from the earlier barren planet, eh?' She cackled, clearly pleased with her own humour.

The Supremo sat still at his desk, toying with a gold paperweight. His eyes flashed golden for one brief moment, at the word banished. When he spoke, his voice was normal, pleasant even.

'Have something to eat, Dhoomavati,' was all he said.

A retinue of silent staff brought in trays of food that covered the entire length of the large, twenty-seater table.

Dhoomavati uttered a little shriek. Without speaking a word, she seemed to carve through the mountain of food. She didn't just gorge, she devoured. Her toothless mouth opened wide as she shovelled food in, indiscriminately and without any pleasure. In no time, the emaciated old woman stood in front of a sea of empty dishes and belched loudly. Then she opened her mouth wide and simply sucked in the whole table with the empty dishes. She looked as underfed and hungry as ever when she finally turned to face Kali.

Archly, she said, 'I see your obsession with gold still carries on. Maybe you should've made yourself a gold suit with the braiding in black instead. Now, why did you send Dreadful Durukti to abduct me?'

'You forget that I *am* gold, Dhoomavati,' replied

Kali calmly. 'And all the vices too,' he added, nodding towards the cigarette stub on the carpet. 'Which is why you worship me more than you know, and I have my power over you just like I do over every other being on Earth.'

'The great Mahesh made me this way and I serve his grand purpose. If he needed me to be a nurturing goddess at this time, you would have seen me as Kamala. The time for dissolution is near; I have had to change myself.'

'Brazen words Dhoomavati, but your eyes betray your doubt. It can't be easy, being abandoned like this. All beings on Earth are under my sway now. Why don't you join the side where the power lies?'

'*Almost* all beings,' snapped Dhoomavati. 'There are still people wed to the better principles of humanity. And their day is coming.'

'A negligible minority,' shrugged Kali. 'The rest can be bought or seduced or imprisoned. Gold, money, prostitutes, alcohol, drugs, power—I rule them all. This epoch is all mine, and don't you forget it.'

'Your epoch, as you put it Kali, is ripe for dissolution. Have I not told you before? Shambhal has fulfilled its destiny; the child has been born.'

'Are you sure?' asked Vikokh in his crisp voice.

She spun on her toes to face him, noticing him for the first time. 'Why the devil should I answer to *you*, minion? Know this, Kali—the avatar was born when the Sun, Moon and Jupiter were in Pushya nakshatra in Karkata. That was nearly fourteen years ago. This child is still safe and secure and hidden and it is now fourteen years of age.'

'Is it male or female?' persisted Vikokh, in the same crisp voice.

A subtle change came over her expression, like an invisible hood. She hesitated for a fraction of a second. In the pod, they all felt it.

'I don't know,' was all she said. 'All I know is that this child will challenge and overthrow the existing order.'

'Where is the child now? Who looks after it? Who are its parents?'

Again, they felt the same reticence. Then she spoke. 'As I said before, the child is hidden well, and away from its birth parents. It will move all over, as is its destiny. You can try to find Shambhal, for a start. Some say it's in the Ganga valley, or near the Chengapattanam–Andhraka region; or maybe it's where the Buddhist Shambhal is—close to Tibet. Others have another name for it—Shangri-La.' She leered with glee at Vikokh. 'You magician boys have your work cut out for you, don't you?'

Then she disappeared in a whiff of smoke, leaving behind the dying fragments of her malicious laughter.

'Well, gentlemen?' enquired the Supremo after a pause, with a lift of his heavy eyebrows. 'How far will your sorcery skills take us?'

Vikokh walked up to the white carpet—now spotted with ash and sporting an unsightly burn—and knelt down. From his breast pocket, he took out a pair of forceps and a small envelope. Then with an obsessive fastidiousness, he picked up the cigarette stub and put it in the envelope. These were then deposited back into his breast pocket with infinite care.

Without turning from the task at hand, he asked his brother, 'Did you notice the pause before her answer when I queried her on the gender of the Enemy?'

'Was she hiding something, you mean?' replied his twin almost immediately. Their quick and complete comprehension of each other was one of the reasons behind the brothers' invincible partnership.

'That could be it … she could also be unsure of the importance of what she knew, or she could be in the middle of interpreting something … but there is something she is not telling us.'

'Pity we can't coerce her into it,' interjected the Supremo. 'She can be tricked or bribed, of course.

Try food. Dhoomavati was born from a curse and is perpetually starving. If there's any shred of information on the child, I want it.'

'With your permission, Supremo, we'll borrow the cigarette stub for analysis and an insight into Dhoomavati's thoughts. You'll have the report when we're done,' said Vikokh.

General Kokh cleared his throat, formally stood to attention and said: 'As far as the search for the Enemy goes, Supremo, we have no choice but to start a hunt for this child. For a start, in the places that Dhoomavati mentioned, and then we'll spread outwards from there, if necessary. I shall immediately put our two agents on Earth on the job.'

'May victory be with you, gentlemen. You will find yourselves directly above your residence when you leave the pod,' said the Supremo, standing up and indicating that the session was over.

The twins clicked their heels, bowed, turned and dissolved through the walls to the spot they had left earlier in the evening. Neither mentioned it, of course, but both felt the acute relief of leaving the Supremo's presence. Ten minutes longer in that confined space and they both knew that they would have collapsed from the stench.

Lakshmi Menon sat at her desk, deep in thought. Her job here was done. Her own mother had sworn allegiance to the wordkeepers in her time, and she had fulfilled her part today. Her role in this would be traced soon enough, she supposed. She didn't expect to have an easy time evading her enemies. But that was no reason to give up.

She briskly made her plans for escape. It took her half an hour to decide a route, withdraw money and prepare for departure. Only a completely new identity would suffice. Lakshmi Menon would have to die.

As she stepped out of the bank into the afternoon sunshine, she attempted to look carefree. She was doing fine, too, until two men in suits and Aviator sunglasses walked up on either side of her. Before she could protest, she was neatly manoeuvered into a waiting sedan.

The black car silently drove out of the portico, the security guard smartly saluting it on its way. Inside, Lakshmi Menon sat paralysed, as Anrit and Nirritti assumed their normal shapes and drove her to their centre of operations.

THE LETTER

Dear Anya,

If you're reading this, you probably know that I am in grave danger, if not already dead.

I have passed on a mantle of great responsibility to you. I wish it could have been otherwise, Anya, but there is no such thing as a normal life for one born into a wordkeeper's clan, as you are. For you to understand all this, I have to go back many thousands of years, to the end of the Mahabharat war—the terrible Kurukshetra.

There are cycles of four yugs in the lifetime of this Earth— Satya, Treta, Dwapar and Kali—each one lasting for about five to eight thousand years, as mentioned in the ancient texts. Each yug declines a little bit more in moral fibre and in the quality of human existence. It is as if the proportion of evil increases in our hearts and on our Earth with the passing years. Time after time, to redress this imbalance and put all of us back on the path of honesty and justice, the avatar appears on Earth. I don't really know if he is Lord Vishnu, but I caught a glimpse of him once and he does exist. In this set of four eons, he is supposed to come in ten different guises or avatars. Nine of these avatars have already arrived and saved humankind in their own time. Kalki, his tenth form, is yet to manifest.

The Kurukshetra war happened at the end of the Dwapar Yug, when Krishna himself predicted that he would come in the next yug as the Gautam Buddha and then as his final avatar, Kalki. He would sweep through the Earth, ridding her of her corruption, greed and injustice in violent, bloody struggles, until the Earth was cleansed and ready for the next age of righteousness—the next Satya Yug. It was a scary prophecy for many, and there was an utmost need for secrecy in all the details of his coming. A secret band was set up to carry the word from generation to generation, until the time was right.

These were the wordkeepers, hereditary guardians of the prophecy, entrusted with locating and finding him when he came. Krishna himself split his blood-red Syamantak gem into ten parts and gave one to each wordkeeper as an identifier to be carried with them and passed on to their children, so they would know each other through the generations. Unfortunately, the prophecy was betrayed by one of us almost immediately. And that is where the trouble began.

Kali Yug, that is, the eon that we live in right now is named after an actual god called Kali (not the Goddess Kaali). A fallen god, more base demon than anything else, but a god nonetheless, with his own divine powers. Krishna's prophecy about the tenth avatar included one important part—that the avatar would cause an apocalyptic end to this eon by slaying Kali and ending this yug with his death. Our Earth would then be rebuilt on the foundations of truth and justice.

One of the first wordkeepers let this slip after drinking too much at an Indraprasth tavern (Indraprasth used to be the capital of the Pandavs). He was found the next morning, with his throat slit from ear to ear. Luckily, he had the good sense to keep the amulet behind with his wife.

Since then, Kali has relentlessly pursued the wordkeepers, trying to wipe us out and to acquire the amulets, which, he believes, will render him victorious. Our clans have, therefore, had to go underground. We are of different nationalities, different faiths and different races. We exist across the globe and pursue different callings. Yet we all have the same agenda—to discover the tenth avatar with the help of the Chiranjeevi, to protect and serve him.

Your first task will be to go to Asirgarh, to find the Chiranjeevi. From there, you will be directed to the other wordkeepers.

Unfortunately, that is all I know myself. I don't know what the Chiranjeevi looks like, but look for the person who worships at the Shiva temple at Asirgarh Fort every morning—people have reported seeing a fresh rose every day at the shrine.

They don't know who leaves it there. The worshipper has never been seen, even though the rose has been there every day for many centuries.

The tenth avatar was born this year, Anya—just like you—and if I'm not there, then it becomes your life's mission to discover him, protect him and join him when he's ready. I am forbidden by our laws to reveal any more at this stage. Perhaps the others will, if you find them. It is a path fraught with great danger and many betrayals, but at stake is a better, truer world.

Take care, my darling! Succeed where I have failed. I would much rather have taken on this difficult task myself, but the fates have decreed otherwise. Remember that I'll always, always love you. Vijayi bhava—be victorious.

Ma

November 2014

THE CHIRANJEEVI

Anya folded the letter and stared out of the window, her head a whirl of emotions. She didn't want to be a part of this crazy quest. All she wanted was normalcy, and all the normal problems and comforts that came with teenage life.

Instead of which, she had to find a messiah and face all kinds of trouble from nameless enemies in the process. For what? For some mythical person or creature who probably doesn't exist in the first place? Tears of resentment pricked her eyes. *Why me? Why couldn't she just leave me alone?*

The passenger sitting opposite was watching her keenly from behind his shawl. His eyes were the only part of his face that were visible, burning bright in the shadows. Anya carefully scrutinised him while pretending to read the railway notice behind the man's head. He was a large man, at least that much was sure. Even sitting, his head nearly touched the bunk above. In spite of herself, she found herself staring at his strange toes.

She looked outside the window. The train was passing through a coconut plantation, its rhythmic chugging making her drowsy. Her lids half closed in spite of her attempts to keep them open. She dozed off.

She saw her mother. Ma in a red land, with red earth and red rocks and a red and black flag. The flag had an emblem on it. An eagle … no wait, an owl. It fluttered from a high stone tower and she found herself soaring up, up towards it, closer and closer ...

Anya, Anya, Anya darling—
I'm coming Ma, I'll save you, just keep—

I'm being watched.

Like a trickle of cold water, the realisation gradually seemed to seep down into her warm cocoon of sleep.

A face was hovering near the window, close to her line of vision. No, not a face, an eye. A green eye with sandy lashes, a GIGANTIC eye, filling her entire window and it had just flashed in recognition.

Anya felt the shock jolt her awake. Cold air thrashed at her cheeks and she realised she was not on the train anymore, but flying through the air, through a mist of clouds that shrouded her. A huge man—no, thing—held her tightly in both hands as she struggled fruitlessly against him. She might as well have been a newspaper rustling in the wind. He shook her once, his claws digging into her skin, making her bones rattle. She slumped into surrender, deciding to conserve her energy for later.

She half saw, half felt the monster's wings beating against the sky. He had the face of a man and the body of a bird. Tiny droplets stung her face as they sped through the clouds. A brilliant, yellow flash rang past her ears, falling to the ground in a graceful arc, setting fire to a section of the coconut plantation. More flashes narrowly swept past them immediately after. They were being attacked.

Her captor rose higher in the air. Her ears were ringing. She could no longer see anything, not even light. For a few moments, she was in excruciating pain from the cold, but before she had time to collect her thoughts, they had landed.

They were on the turret of a ruined fort; it was spread out like a sleeping giant in a forest—for here, nature had won over human endeavour in the end. Civilisation could be seen in the distance, but Anya knew she was too far away for anyone to see or hear her. Screaming would be futile. She turned to her captor—or was it her rescuer?

Unsure of what lay ahead, she asked, 'What do you want? To kill me?'

'You are now at Asirgarh Fort, wordkeeper. I thought I'd help you to get here faster than your enemies would allow. The Chiranjeevi will meet you here.'

'You saved me. Why?'

The man's face became inscrutable. His eyes flickered once. 'I was ordered to do it,' he said simply.

'Wait!' she said, desperate for company and answers. 'Who are you? Who ordered you?'

'I am a yaksha, a nature guardian. You must ask me no more, I am bound to silence.'

'By whom? Can't you tell me anything more about this?'

The yaksha hesitated, measuring his words. He wants to help me without breaking his vow, thought Anya.

'There is talk in my world about a secret weapon that will destroy who you are seeking.'

'Destroy whom? The avatar? What does this weapon look like?'

'Anything can be a weapon. The main thing is the heart that wants to use it, wordkeeper. Find the heart that wishes to destroy.'

'Thanks for helping me.'

The yaksha's face twisted into an odd expression.

With a quick wave at Anya, he swiftly rose into the air and vanished.

Anya shivered in her wet clothes and swore. It had been three days of waiting. She was sitting behind a tree near the Shiva temple, where the Chiranjeevi was supposed to come every morning. So far, luck had eluded her. To save herself the embarrassment of being stared at by passersby, she had chosen a secluded spot from where she could observe the entrance to the temple, but not be seen herself. And for three frustrating days, she had seen only ordinary worshippers come and go. The lone red rose left at the entrance every day continued to mock her vigil.

She shifted uncomfortably in her filthy jeans and thought once again about her strange escape, partly to take her mind off the discomfort. The memory of the giant eye terrified her still. What *was* that? She was sure of one thing, though: it looked human. Whoever the owner of that eye was, he or she was several hundred times larger and could move at the speed of a running train. Or was it just a single eye, magicked into following her? Was it still watching her here at the Shiva temple, waiting for an opportune moment? Anya was so carried away with her own thoughts that she didn't realise she was muttering to herself.

'It's a search eye; trained like a hound. It starts to hunt its quarry after an initial scan of its appearance or photograph,' a voice close to her whispered. A different voice this time; not the one that had spoken to her at Bangalore.

Anya jumped, then looked around, fearful of being discovered, but there was no one near her. The voice seemed to come from thin air. Cautious of being overheard, she whispered, 'Who is this?'

'The one you're looking for.'

'Where are you? Why can't I see you?'

'If I appear, you might scream and that would alert the devotees. I do not wish to be discovered.'

'I won't scream,' Anya whispered again.

The air in front of her shimmered like a curtain. Bit by little bit, it seemed to solidify in the smoky shape of a man. In front of her astonished eyes, colour filled the shape. The giant from her dream was standing between her and the temple, blocking her view, a bitter half-smile on his face. It would have been a handsome face, but for an ugly suppurating sore on his forehead the size of a car headlight. She stuffed her fist into her mouth to stop herself from screaming.

'Hullo Anya,' said the giant in impeccable English, his pleasant baritone contrasting oddly with the primitive surroundings and that terrifying face.

Excerpt from *The Times of India*

26 May 2028

Press Trust of India The Indian Government has been deposed on grounds of 'inefficiency and corruption' by a Supreme Council of generals. In a televised address, their leader, the Supremo, said: 'We were compelled to rid the Indian state of its current crop of leaders and politicians due to persistent corruption and a lack of commitment to economic growth. Parliament has been disbanded and the Constitution annulled. New laws are being devised for the nation, under the able leadership of industrialist Rajanipati Khetawat, who will be the country's prime minister from this day on.'

There is no information on the whereabouts of the former prime minister or the members of the erstwhile Cabinet.

Notice in All National Dailies

27 May 2028

Police are looking for Anya Sharma, 14, in connection with the disappearance of her mother, Tanya Sharma. Anya is 5′5″, has a wheatish complexion and is slim. She was last seen in blue jeans and a white t-shirt. A reward of Rs 5,00,000 is hereby announced for information leading to her capture. Anya is dangerous, and probably armed.

Excerpt from *The Deccan Herald*

31 May 2028

Lakshmi Menon, Manager of Vaults, Bank of Baroda, Magyar Road. Menon had been arrested and suspended by the recently created Security Council on charges of professional impropriety. The motives behind her allowing an unaccompanied minor to operate a vault were being investigated by Bangalore Police. Menon was last seen on the night of 28 May 2028, as she left the police station after her interview. Her body was recovered from the Company Gardens Tank yesterday by an attendant. Menon is survived by her husband.

PART TWO

PART TWO

Notes from an Immortal

I, Vibhishan, past Lord of the Sinhala land of Lanka, immortal by the grace of my Lord Ram, and the general of the wordkeepers, write the following.

A yaksha this time. It carried off the wordkeeper in a whirl, as a gigantic tracker eye spotted her. For an instant, I thought my eldest brother had something to do with the whole thing. Yakshas are very much his style. But he had been so aloof from the struggle for so long that I could find no connection. People say he's amassed untold wealth, they worship him for it—an indicator of the times we live in. He was never worshipped in the other yugs. Perhaps he's joined forces with Kali in their quest for even more wealth. I can't vouch for him; we hardly stayed in touch.

They could fly and I couldn't, so I watched her fly off towards the northwest. The Seer had told me the wordkeeper would overcome all obstacles and that was my only consolation. Not that I could rely on the Seer. Word on the street (the streets immortals like me roam, that is) was that she had been seen with the enemy and peddled her Sight to both sides for food or according to her whim. How the mighty have fallen! Her ability to See was still intact, but her indifference to our struggle has hurt us over the centuries. Two hundred years ago, when the great betrayal came, she could have warned us. She chose, instead, to remain silent, and we lost three of our own.

With the wordkeeper gone, I am the only one left to seek my lord. And I am hopelessly at a loss, a blind general. Will there never be an ally?

BILAL

B ilal ran as fast as he could, but the crease still seemed miles away. He had underestimated the fielder at mid-on and asked for the second run. In desperation, he leaped for the chalky white line, his bat thrust out fully, and landed with a painful thud on his front. The amulet around his neck thumped loudly as it hit his collarbone.

The roar of an appeal could be heard in the air. Bilal shook himself up and looked at the leg umpire, a boy like himself. A pause, then a shake of the head. Saved!

He had played cricket on this dusty little pitch for as long as he could remember. His set of playmates had also remained the same. All that had changed over the years was their height. Rafiq was the boys' captain and his closest friend. There were also Ismail, Chhotu and Madan.

Bilal's village consisted of Hindus and Muslims in roughly equal proportions. The undercurrents of mutual suspicion were there, but so was the daily cricket match.

Today was not Bilal's day. His knock of thirty off thirty-four balls was useful, but not enough. Easwar's team carried the day with Govind's unbeaten fifty. Bilal had to be satisfied with a consolation pat on the back from his captain, as he put marigold leaves on the cut on his knee. The boys limped dejectedly back homewards.

Bilal's village was in the heartlands of Andhra Pradesh. A good two decades ago, it had been in the grip of Naxalite rule and no one from the outside world dared to step in. Times had changed since then and now the main road boasted electric lights; the villagers had found weaving and agriculture a more attractive proposition than guns after the state government had introduced a slew of welfare measures.

Not everything was so wonderful about peace, though. Bilal had to go to school under the new development norms set by UNICEF—not just give his attendance and scoot for the rest of the day like the earlier generation bragged they did, but really attend. He sometimes half wished for the old, violent times he had heard about.

'Oye! Bilal!' shouted a reedy voice from the other side of the makeshift bridge. 'Look what I've got here!'

It was Bablu, the postman's son. His father had recently got a shiny new bicycle, courtesy the District Post Office, and Bilal had taken a few spins on it as a special privilege, being Bablu's friend.

Bablu was in a state of high excitement. His eyes bulging more than usual, he waved a glossy leaflet at them. It was an ultra-colourful, shiny piece of paper that said: 'India's Most Talented: 2028' and 'Let US find you!' in big, bold letters. The same message was again repeated in Telegu and Urdu, the two local languages.

'They're coming here, our district, then all villages,' said Bablu in one long breath, beside himself with excitement. 'And they'll hold auditions, we can all go, we can be on TV, imagine!'

The boys were immediately galvanised into action. Fevered discussions were held on gymnastics, gym displays and cycling tricks. Madan offered to sing, for he had a pleasant voice, but this offer found no takers. Music was too tame. Rope tricks, suggested someone. No, a play with all the rest thrown in, said someone else. Chattering happily, the boys disappeared into the dusk.

Rukhsana sat, worried, her rosy-cheeked visage marred by a single crease on her forehead. As always, it was her son she was fretting about. Boys were so tiresome, so annoyingly immature! How Bilal would take on his responsibilities, god alone knew. Had he been a girl, he'd be managing half the household by now. And there he was, still playing cricket and lying about doing his homework. Anyway, she would be having a chat with him about his goals soon enough. His fourteenth birthday was less than a month away.

Rukhsana got up and washed her face and hands, taking a cursory look at the mirror in front of her. A pahari woman, she was used to standing out in this village. She had met Bilal's father years ago, when he had migrated to Uttar Pradesh in search of a job. His own state was still in turmoil and a weaver could get employment around Benares if he tried, so he had moved, like many others from his area. They had fallen in love, married and returned fourteen years ago, with baby Bilal in tow. Rukhsana had changed her faith and had given up her old name. It was a completely new existence for the mountain woman, but she was so in love with Bilal's father that she didn't look back even once. Her evident sincerity had eventually won over her new neighbours, although they still couldn't stomach her cooking.

Hearing a knock on the door, she hastened towards it. Expecting her son or husband, she didn't cover her face, as was the custom among Muslim women here.

The man who entered was neither. He was a pahari like her, clean-shaven, with ash stripes on his forehead; a voice from her distant past and dreaded future.

'Salaam, Rukhsana begum,' he said with a smile. 'Or should I still call you Uma?'

'I am Rukhsana now,' she said firmly, pretending to a courage she didn't feel. 'What do you want, Kaka?'

'The boy is old enough to be returned to us, Rukhsana begum,' said the man. 'When can I take him with me?'

'He's not fourteen yet, Kaka—there's still a month to go—is this not too soon?'

'The times are dangerous; your boy needs to be equipped to deal with these times and his own special destiny. We will train him to do so. You understood all of this when he was entrusted to you as a baby. You cannot back out now,' persisted the man.

'Give me a month,' pleaded Rukhsana desperately. 'At least let me prepare him for this.'

'Very well, I shall be back in thirty days. Let me see, he should be fourteen years and three days old by then,' replied the man, stepping back into the darkness.

Rukhsana was left alone in the house again, but fear was now her constant companion.

Rafiq and Bilal walked together towards their huts. The boys lived next to each other and this was a daily routine. The moon hung low over the terracotta tiled roofs that could be seen in a ghostly outline up ahead.

'Why don't we do your trick?' asked Rafiq, keeping his voice low. 'You can do it any time you want.'

'Which trick?' Bilal's voice was light.

'The one you showed me. You know, the one in which you vanish from one spot and reappear in another.'

'Oh that!' Bilal's soft laugh could be heard in the still night. 'That's just a silly magician's game—anyone can do that.'

'No, magicians use boxes and screens and stuff—they don't really vanish, like you do. And anyway, it's miles better than what the others are thinking of doing. We could mix it in with the other stuff, if you like. If we do it we could win, easy.'

'I'd rather not, Rafiq, I don't want the village to hunt me down for black magic, thanks,' said Bilal, sounding uncomfortable.

'We'll make it look like any other magic trick, then,' persisted Rafiq. 'We'll put in one of those boxes magicians use on stage, only ours won't have special hidden places, 'cause you won't need them. Then it won't seem all that strange.'

Not for the first time, Bilal cursed his childish impulse to show off. His Ammi had repeatedly forbidden him to ever talk of his special gift. 'They'll not understand, Bilal. You think it's just a game, but it scares people. They fear what they don't understand, and I don't want you hurt. You'll have to resist the temptation to tell people about this.'

Well, he'd not been able to resist. One quiet afternoon, while he and Rafiq were hiding from the other boys during a game of 'ice-pice', he had sworn Rafiq to silence and had shown him the trick.

Now this.

'All right, we'll put it in,' he sighed. 'But you'll have to tell the others that the box has a hiding place, and that I'll unlock it from inside and escape. And not a word to Ammi,' he warned, a panicky note creeping into his voice.

'Will do, dost,' grinned Rafiq. 'At least we'll have a chance to come on TV with your trick; just imagine everyone's face when we do.' His teeth gleamed white in the moonlight, as he smiled and waved, before turning towards his house.

'Ammi, I'm home,' shouted Bilal.

A week had gone by. The boys had arrived at their idea after much squabbling. Their five-minute routine now consisted of a play, which would include Madan's song, Bablu's bicycle tricks (on his father's cycle, of course), a gym display by the rest and Bilal's disappearing act as a climax. Everyone was happy at last, except Bilal, and rehearsals were in full swing. Cricket had been completely forgotten as the auditions were only a week away.

Bilal had figured out his own routine. It involved diving inside the box, which would then be wheeled behind a screen, and disappearing from his hiding place, so that the audience would find an empty box when it was reopened. He would, of course, reappear in the middle of the audience and take his bow. Nothing resembling a real miracle that would start a nationwide discussion, just a neat little magic trick.

Meanwhile, the district town was agog with excitement. The talent hunt had finally set shop in their midst. A ramshackle warehouse had been given a new lick of paint and now sung out in garish colours:

INDIA'S MOST TALENTED
HAVE YOU GOT WHAT IT TAKES?

Santhosh, the district coordinator, a young man in a blue shirt, was frowning as he read through the list of applicants. 'Hmm, rope trick, rope trick, singing, classical dance, more singing, even more singing, acrobatics, a magic play, western dance ...' He circled 'magic play' and 'acrobatics' as he read. Then he put up a final list on the notice board outside and pushed through the incoming swell of people who were rushing to see if their names figured.

'We're there!' squealed an excited voice within the sea of heads. 'Madan, did you see that? We made it to the audition!' Bablu's voice was now a reedy falsetto.

The boys ran out of the milling crowd and pedalled away furiously on Bablu's father's bicycle, which had been requisitioned for their use without the postman's knowledge.

THE TALENT HUNT

Santhosh looked doubtfully at the straggly group of boys in front of him. Perhaps the western dance candidate would have been a better choice, after all. This group seemed to have no leader; they all screeched at the top of their voices, desperate to explain how wonderful their idea was, to the smart man from TV.

'Hold on, hold on; let's just have one person speaking. Why don't you explain?' he nodded at a relatively older boy, hoping that he would show more maturity than the others.

Rafiq cleared his throat and began. 'Well, it's like this, see—the story's about a wicked wizard taking the little orphan princess prisoner, so he can rule over the kingdom and take all her money. Then there's this boy, see, who ...'

'With his friends, with his friends!' screamed three shrill voices in unison.

'On a cycle!' screeched a fourth voice.

And it began all over again.

The coordinator took a deep breath and tried again. 'Well, why don't you boys show me what you've got, and I'll let you know if there are any changes to be made, all right?'

The makeshift stage was suddenly a hub of all sorts of activity. The boys put together props, boxes and screens in record time. To the coordinator's surprise, they were quite good. There was a princess who sang (Madan), a tooth-gnashing villain (Rafiq), the hero (Bilal) with his band of acrobatic friends, one of whom could ride a bicycle in a variety of ways (Bablu). The climax was a magic trick that allowed the trapped hero to escape and emerge, triumphant, amongst the audience.

I've struck TRP gold, he thought.

The show would be aired over thirteen weeks, and showcase each of the shortlisted groups across the country. Four semifinalists would be chosen for a separate segment, which would then determine two finalists and, after another round, the national winner. The episodes would be shot simultaneously across the country by several teams. The national coordinator would put together the rest.

Santhosh was itching to tell his superiors about this little local find. But instead he wrapped up the rehearsal, said a quick 'Well done' to the boys, and gave them their final shooting schedule for the following day.

As the excited group filtered out, he saw one boy, the villainous wizard, hesitate for a moment, as if he wished to say something. But by the time Santhosh figured that out, Rafiq had left.

'Bilal, I need you to wake up early tomorrow,' said Ammi. 'I'm taking you to the dargah first thing in the morning.'

'But Ammi, I have rehearsals then,' protested the boy, his mouth full of dinner.

'That's enough, son,' said Rukhsana in a voice that indicated she would brook no opposition. 'Your Abbu and I are taking you, and you're coming. You don't turn fourteen every day.'

Bilal got up from the floor, taking his steel plate with him. I always do as I'm told, he grumbled to himself. But why is it that when I need some time for my own hobbies, nobody listens? I could go to the dargah in the afternoon, after everything else. He scrubbed hard at his plate with ash, until it shone dully in the moonlight.

The face appeared, as if from nowhere. The plate reflected high cheekbones, narrow eyes and grey, cropped hair. Bilal turned in a flash, some animal instinct inside him ready for attack. But the man simply smiled.

'Bilal miah, shall we meet near the village bridge in two hours? Let me see, it will be past midnight then, and you will be all of fourteen years old,' he said.

'Who are you? What do you want?' whispered Bilal.

'That's what we need to talk about,' said the man. 'Come alone and don't tell your parents.'

'That's impossible,' Bilal said flatly. 'I do nothing without their knowledge.'

'Ever wondered why you look so different from everyone else?' said the man, and melted into the darkness.

It was a sultry night, with a nearly full moon throwing a silvery light on everything. No one saw Bilal creep out silently and head towards the field. He stopped at the ramshackle bridge where the village ended and the fields began. The stranger was outlined in the distance by the light of the moon. He beckoned to Bilal and they sat under a nearby mulberry tree.

The man began speaking in his soothing, soft tones. How he came from a mountain village in the north; how times were changing in the outside world and how good, meek people everywhere were being left behind for the insatiable greed of some.

'It is not like these people who are unjust are a small rag-tag bunch. There is now a vast, powerful majority, carrying out an untold number of wrongdoings just because power is on their side. They can change governments. They ARE the government. They are changing age-old laws to suit their lust for more money, more power. Good people are being disallowed from challenging them by the laws they are passing. And they are doing this across the world, not just in our land. Which is the beginning for worse to come.'

'So?' asked Bilal, stifling a yawn, playing with his stone amulet as he listened without much interest.

His companion smiled. 'There has always been a prophecy among my people about a saviour of the deserving. Signs were predicted by our greatest scholars and historical documents talked about how this saviour would restore justice to us all. The great day came, exactly fourteen years ago.' He looked meaningfully at the boy sitting next to him.

Bilal half-choked and half-laughed. 'Me? You mean me? Why am I the one? What about all the other children born on the same day? Have you gone and met them all?'

'We did check, Bilal. But there was only one new-born baby in Shambhal that night. And that was you.'

'Where is this place that you talk about, this Shambhal? Is it near Dharamsala? Ammi says her people were from Dharamsala.'

'It's a secret location, son. But surely, you can tell you're from some other land. Take a look at yourself. How many children in this village do you know who are as fair as you?'

Bilal looked down at his reflection in the muddy, moonlit river. The man was right. He was fair, very fair. If it hadn't been for his dark eyes and dark hair, people would have naturally taken him to be a white tourist.

The man continued, 'We even know about your special power. Why, you disappeared on us once while we were bringing you back from Shambhal and we had a hard time searching for you, until you reappeared on time for your next feed.' He laughed softly. 'As you've probably guessed, your parents are not your real parents. You were removed from them for your safety. You have some very powerful enemies, son, and we have tried our utmost to keep you hidden away until you are strong enough to face them. We now feel the time is right for you to gain training in the political realities of this land and in martial arts. And I have come to take you.'

'But I can't go,' Bilal blurted out. 'I don't want to leave my parents, my village, my friends. What if

I don't want to be this great saviour? I just want to play cricket and do what all the other children do. I won't go.'

'I can't force you, Bilal,' said the man, shaking his head. 'But you have no idea of your potential yet. I am going to be around for a month in case you change your mind.'

Bilal stood up. Sticking his chin out, he said firmly, 'Well, I won't. Khuda hafiz.'

Nirritti yawned and tried to concentrate on the task at hand. Her cover on this job was national coordinator, and in hindsight, she was sure it was a mistake. Anrit and she had devised a talent hunt competition, hoping it would throw up exceptional, possibly divine abilities from across India, and thereby allow them to carry out a search for any suspicious phenomena. An excuse to mobilise a 'needle in a haystack' search. But she had not factored in the amount of footage she would have to go through. Spotting a miracle needed an eye that was well versed in magic. The sheer dreariness of her job had started sapping even her inexhaustible reserves of energy.

There were other covert searches in place: nationwide IQ tests in education for anyone off the charts, competitions to determine superhuman physical or sporting ability and an international circus event, which would throw up any extraordinary talent. Anrit coordinated those and from their daily discussions, his job wasn't any easier.

She disconnected the hard drive she was viewing and put in a fresh one. It was the last of the recorded preliminary rounds. This one was from Andhra Pradesh. There was the usual share of music performances. An average talent, music. Many people were blessed with a basic ability to sing or play an instrument. Those who pursued it diligently achieved proficiency. But sparks of genius were especially few and miraculous musical performers, nonexistent. No, music is not where we'll find our quarry, she thought.

She rose to fetch another cup of coffee and had her back turned to her screen when the next show came on. A play was in progress. Stray dialogues about a wizard reached her ears. Curious, she headed back to her desk.

Hmm. First promising lead of the day. An ensemble cast performed an acrobatic play, which was rounded off with a disappearing trick. She filed it away under her 'Round 2' dossier. Every detail would be needed, to find out how the group managed to do it. In the meantime, they would move up to the next level so they could be watched.

Bilal and his troupe were now part of a motley crew consisting of a knife swallower, a fire walker, a girl who could light lamps with her singing and the fastest under-fourteen keyboardist in the world.

Meanwhile, the boys were ecstatic. Their success in the preliminary round meant they could now participate at the state level. Ideas were running thick and fast, mostly on upping the ante by one notch. The songs would have to be better—maybe some musical accompaniments? The acrobatics would need new, more daring acts. And Bilal's magic trick—well, every one conceded that that was the one factor allowing them to really stand out, so it would have to be really, *really* good. Bilal would have to think of something extra special ...

Bilal nodded absently and walked away from the rest of them. He had told them he was learning magic tricks from a magician in the next village and the others didn't suspect. Only Rafiq knew that he could do much more than vanish and reappear, because Bilal had confided in him a few days ago. A voice inside his head said, go on, you've always wanted people to notice you and it's not like they know you're using your gift. But what if he got found out?

'Oye! Bilal!' Rafiq caught up with him, panting hard after running the whole way. 'Idea. Ali Baba!'

'What?' said Bilal. Sometimes Rafiq made no sense.

'Story ... Ali Baba ... next play ...' gasped Rafiq between breaths. 'You do the "simsim" bit.'

'You mean open and shut the cave doors?'

'That, and the other stuff. The things inside the cave—all the gold and silver bits must look real.'

'But why not make them?' asked Bilal, although he knew the answer beforehand. Making was a lot more expensive. Plus, it would never look as good. 'I don't want Ammi to know I've done anything here,' he added.

'That's the beauty of it. No one will. Madan can play Ali Baba, you see. You'll just stay in the background and do your stuff.'

Bilal was not too happy with this arrangement. A secret part of him wanted very much to be noticed. He was actually hoping Rafiq would cajole him some more to do the stunts and then he'd graciously give in. Then, when the audience clapped, he'd just smile a wry smile and say, 'Ladies and gentlemen, it wouldn't have been possible without my friends ...'

Then he imagined his mother's angry face and thought better of it. Best to be a part of the fun without the trouble.

'All right, but you manage the boys,' he said. 'I don't want them to suspect anything.'

Rafiq just waved his hand as he ran back, too excited to talk.

Bilal got up from his bed and silently tiptoed out of the house. The full moon night was convenient for practising his stuff in the play. He walked till he reached the river bank, and sat down in a corner. He closed his eyes. Concentrate now. Think of gold coins, gold coins spilling out of earthen pots ... now one more pot full of gold ... now one more .....

'Busy getting rich, Bilal miah?' said a voice close to his ear.

Jolted out of his thoughts, Bilal opened his eyes to see three urns full of golden coins around him.

'What are you doing here and why are you disturbing me?' he hissed at the man who had come to take him away.

'Some may say that these gifts were meant to help everyone, not yourself,' the man continued, unperturbed.

'They are for everyone. I'm creating props for our play,' Bilal snapped.

'Cheap theatrics? Do you really feel it's the best

use of your talents? Why do you want to get known for the wrong reasons?'

'I didn't ask you for your opinion,' said Bilal.

'Suit yourself, son. But no good will come of this frivolous use of your gift. Be careful.'

The man got up and headed towards the village, not turning back even once.

Good, thought Bilal bitterly. I don't want you to have grand expectations of me. I'm an ordinary boy and I choose an ordinary life.

Nirritti made sure she was personally present at each of the shortlisted events. She had already visited the knife swallower's show and was severely disappointed. Just a routine street-side performance, no more, no less. The singer showed promise, though. She had managed to bring rain with her second performance. Still, it was not unheard of among musicians in India. Having ordered a close watch on the girl and her family, she had now flown down especially for the play troupe and sat in the first row on the left hand side. She meant to find out what their secret tricks were.

Ali Baba was a clear favourite with the crowd. They loved the singing hero and the acrobatic thieves, who numbered rather less than forty, but the crowd was in a forgiving mood. There were stunts aplenty, but what got her interested were the special effects. An extremely realistic stone cave, pots of gold that looked exactly like gold, that realistic grinding sound of cave doors closing. Pretty darned impossible on a village budget ... She couldn't wait to go backstage, but the play was still on. And then she had to wait for ten more minutes while the troupe took several bows. No one wanted them to leave.

Nirritti raced backstage as soon as the curtains fell.

Nothing. Not one piece of prop. Someone had silently cleaned the whole set out in ten minutes. She rushed out, instructing her staff to keep every backstage recording on her desk.

The boys were melting into the darkness of the village, heading towards their respective homes. She stopped one, the singer who had played Ali Baba. Madan was thrilled to talk to the 'Madam from the show' but couldn't help her, much to his regret. All the direction and the backstage work had been handled by their director, Rafiq. He was the brain behind the whole thing. Nirritti flashed the boy a smile that dazzled him. Madan had to sit down and catch his breath after she left.

Rafiq came upon the lady just before he reached the river bank. He couldn't take his eyes off her. She smelt so lovely, looked so beautiful, and when she spoke to him in her sweet husky tone, he felt he could tell her everything, whatever she asked.

She was so appreciative. So kind. She said she had really admired the work he had done backstage. For a moment, Rafiq hesitated. But something about Nirritti had turned this village lad into a man all of a sudden. He really wanted to impress her, to tell her it was him all along ... Bilal needn't know. And Bilal was the one who wanted to be anonymous, anyway.

Rafiq told his new admirer about his magical gift, how he could disappear and reappear, how he could make stones move, how he could ... He was just warming up to tell her about the urns of gold when she calmly reached out and snapped his neck in two.

His body lay next to the river, its dead, surprised eyes staring up at the moon.

ENEMY OF THE STATE

Bilal couldn't sleep. The excitement had been too much. His heart had barely stopped racing since the show, and he felt he could run a mile before he'd even feel tired. He silently stepped out of his house.

The moon was high in the sky and his usual haunts were milky and gleaming. He made his way towards the river, intending to cross it and run in the field beyond. That way no one would hear him.

He walked up to the bridge and started to cross, avoiding any creaky planks. Finally, with an impatient sigh, he stepped across the last plank and started to run. Almost immediately, he tripped and fell over something.

Life changed in a flash. Rafiq's face looked up in silent wonder at his friend. He was cold.

'What's happened here?' asked a stern voice next to him.

Instinctively, Bilal protested, even before he turned around: 'It wasn't me, I swear. I-I just arrived, he was dead long before ...' he turned round. The stranger was next to him.

'Hush, Bilal, or people will hear you,' the man said, trying to check the note of hysteria that had crept into Bilal's voice. 'Let me see.'

He sat down and swiftly examined the body, turning it around once. Bilal noticed with a sickening feeling that Rafiq's head swung right back, the top of his head facing the ground. He rushed off and vomited by the river bank.

'At least three hours since he died. His neck's been snapped in two. There are no signs that he had been climbing a tree, so I'll have to say someone did it. The question is, why? Why would anyone want to kill a young boy of fourteen or fifteen? After all, he's not the one in danger, *you* are. So why him? ' The stranger looked Bilal steadily in the eye.

Bilal looked down, unable to hold the man's piercing gaze. Three hours. But that would mean just after the show. Just after he, Bilal, had left.

'Mistaken identity, perhaps? Did he know something, Bilal?'

Bilal found himself whispering his secret—how he'd shown off to Rafiq one afternoon; the idea behind the play; how they wanted it to be better than the last one; and his own role in the last performance.

'This is just the first of the innocents,' said the man. 'You have to disappear. Tonight. Before you get killed and others are killed while they sniff you out. Now.'

Bilal said nothing. He would go. He owed his life to his friend.

They crossed the bridge and walked past the huts; Bilal could see his home. His parents were sleeping inside. He wanted to say goodbye so desperately.

'I'm afraid it won't be possible, Bilal,' said the man, a sad note in his voice. 'Your enemies might be watching. You'll just have to slip away in the darkness.'

Bilal walked on with the stranger, his throat lumpy with unshed tears.

'Where are we going?'

'Mahendra Parbat. You may call me Bhargav Sir. I will be your teacher. But first, there are some things you need to know about the entity who is behind this. One: his name is Kali and he is a god. Two: it has been prophesied that you will kill him, so he is out to kill you first. Three: in these days, when allegiance can actually be bought, Kali, with his promise of gold, is extremely powerful. Leaders of all nations bow to his demands. You do realise, don't you, that you will be hunted from this moment on? You are now officially an enemy of Kali and when you join my camp, you will be one of the many enemies of state that his ragtag governments have been asked to exterminate. But I suppose you were an enemy from the moment you were born, so it makes no difference, really.'

Bilal remained silent. This was a strange, new world, one that he had never known existed.

'The good part,' Bhargav continued, 'is that you have a secret group sworn to protect you. They are called the wordkeepers. You can recognise them by their red stone amulets. Each wordkeeper carries one. Here's mine,' he said, rolling up his sleeve to show a blood-red stone set in silver on his forearm.

'I have one of those, too,' said Bilal, animated for the first time since that evening. 'Ammi gave it to me when I turned ten.'

'Rukhsana is one of us, of course,' said Bhargav. 'Her task was to bring you up, far from prying eyes, until you were ready to be trained for what lay ahead. She has loved you as much as your birth mother would have. Free of the amulet, she can now resume a normal life, hopefully without anyone the wiser.'

They were walking down the village road going north, the moon lighting the dusty path. 'We could fly, but its important you know the way.'

As they walked on, Bhargav explained how he had started this camp a few hundred years ago for boys and men, as an undercover resistance to Kali's ever increasing influence.

'A few hundred years ago? How many?'

'About nine hundred, give or take a few years,' smiled his companion.

'But, that would mean ...'

'That I am unusually long-lived. Yes, I am a Chiranjeevi, one of nine immortals left in this world. We die when the Earth perishes at the end of this yug. But more later.'

He went back to describing his camp, how it tended to people who were being oppressed or persecuted. They provided food, shelter and medicines. Gradually, more boys and girls joined his ranks, until he had to take some drastic measures about the space available. They were building up their small army, waiting until the avatar would be born and ready for training.

'I had to reclaim some land from the coast and move the forest dwellers to this new place, so I could expand the camp. I had to make sure that we never recruited from them ever again, of course, and I prohibited them from returning. Over generations, the camp has become the stuff of legend and no one knows exactly where it is. Which is precisely how I wanted it.'

They had reached a small thicket by the side of

the road, where a jeep was parked. A dark-skinned boy with slicked-back, jet-black hair, slightly older than Bilal, stood in the distance. Seeing Bhargav, he walked up towards them and bowed his head.

'Bilal, meet Zak, Zachary Nigel. He is one of the senior camp coordinators and will be guiding you.'

'Nigel? But isn't that a Christian ...'

'And aren't you a Muslim?' smiled his teacher. 'You, of all people, shouldn't be asking that. Your parentage is unknown to many of us. Your mother is a Hindu, but not much is known about your father, although much is written in the old books. You were born in an unknown place, moved to a Buddhist monastery as a baby and your foster parents raised you as a good Muslim. You belong to all faiths, and it's all the same as far as the struggle is concerned.'

It was morning by the time they reached their camp, halfway up Mahendra Giri. Hiding the jeep in a cleverly camouflaged cave, Nigel guided Bilal deeper into the jungle. After a mile or so, Bilal came upon his new home: a series of tents surrounding a small hut in the centre and about two hundred young people, currently engaged in martial arts lessons.

'Welcome,' said Zak, and smiled.

THE PRISON WITH NO WALLS

Bhargav's camp was organised around his tiny cottage, with the boys' tents pitched around the right semicircle, each one sleeping eight boys. The girls were in tents pitched around the left of his hut. The older ones were in charge of basic discipline and schedule of practice sessions. Each child learnt one martial art, close combat fighting, with and without knives, shooting, archery and the basics of guerrilla warfare. Bhargav was an avowed bachelor and lived alone.

Zak Nigel, although young, was in charge of basic physical training. He took Bilal under his wing and often nodded his appreciation when the boy applied himself. Bilal was still unnerved by his taciturn nature and his maturity, but he couldn't deny that Zak was an excellent teacher.

Other than this, the students attended sessions on reading, writing, mathematics, all sciences, astronomy, cartography and compulsory sessions on what their teacher called 'life skills'.

Life skills was a strange lesson: it covered morality, ethics, questions of metaphysics, animal husbandry, basic medicine, needlework, cooking, driving and the care of automobiles. Bhargav had evidently thought it up in one his more inspired moments. It was hugely popular, however, because this was one lesson where nothing was off limits and questions could be freely asked.

It had been a month since Bilal's arrival and he was proving to be an apt pupil. His reflexes had always been sharp. Now, with regular training, he realised he had a gift for combat. He shot with unerring aim and wielded a mean knife. Although small and slight, he was intuitive and often beat larger opponents at wrestling or the martial arts. It was also obvious to his teacher that the boy had a natural ability to lead. His team members frequently listened to him during group activities. His calm nature made him a natural judge.

One afternoon, after the requisite sessions were over, Bhargav called the boy to his hut. Bilal appeared, looking mildly apprehensive.

'You needn't worry,' his teacher said. 'I just wanted to discuss the next part of your training with you.'

Bilal waited silently.

'Your progress in the martial area has been impressive. You are easily the best student I have had in a long time. I would even go so far as to call you a natural. But there are other battles you'll need to win as well. Given your pace of learning, I think its time to introduce them. There is, of course, a matter of urgency here as well. In short, I need you to be ready as fast as you can. We need you to lead us.'

Bilal looked at his teacher, puzzled. 'I don't understand, sir. Do you mean campaign strategy? But we have lessons for those. What other war can there be?'

His teacher looked at Bilal and smiled. 'Weapons don't win every war, son ... and not all strong people are armed.'

'But we just went through all the guerilla warfare stuff—what was that for then?'

'That is necessary as well, more to defend yourself from the violence of others than to cause violence. But what I'm going to show you today is the weapon that is not a weapon and yet, powerful enough to bend people to one's will. The most dangerous weapon in our enemy's arsenal. The prison with no walls.'

'What is it?'

'Well, it's a prison, son—an extremely effective one. It keeps people locked in, for all their lives sometimes. The lucky ones—very few—manage to get out while there's still time. You are the only one who can rescue these prisoners. It's time you saw what you're up against.'

Bilal looked at him, uncomprehending.

Bhargav didn't say anything else. Holding Bilal by the arm, he closed his eyes. Their forms then became transparent, gradually disappearing. Bilal watched as his opaque hand gradually started showing the road under his feet through it. He never tired of the sensation. He held it up and through it, saw the pipal tree they were crossing. Then the hand vanished altogether, leaving no distinction between his body and the surroundings. Bilal marvelled at his teacher's ability to concentrate. His own mind always seemed to jump from thought to thought, making it a slower process.

They returned to the camp just as it was turning dusk.

'Wipe your tears, Bilal,' was all Bhargav said.

Surprised, Bilal reached up to touch his cheeks

and found them wet. He had no idea he had been sobbing.

'What did we just see?'

'Ourselves. The way Kali wishes us to be.'

Bhargav gave the boy some time to cry; he had never seen what Kali's prisoners could do.

'Meet me in my hut in a few minutes,' he said gently.

When Bilal returned to his teacher, he was sitting in his prayer position, facing his favourite tree, a large sheesham. He turned to look at his pupil, indicating that he should take a seat. Bilal folded his legs in the lotus position and looked at his teacher.

'Questions? You must have a few,' said Bhargav.

'What did we see? Was it real?' Bilal asked, his voice still hoarse with tears. They had wandered through strange landscapes during the day and what they had seen had left a deep and indelible impression on him.

The images jostled each other in Bilal's mind: men destroying one another for money; children killing each other over a game; people selling their souls for gold; the powerful looting the powerless; whole villages burnt in ridiculously petty battles of revenge and hatred ... And through it all, a complete lack of guilt or remorse.

'They were like animals,' Bilal whispered.

'No, animals never kill for reasons other than hunger. The people you saw killed for envy, for small victories, for petty revenge, for wealth and power; animals don't do that.'

'Yes, but why? What was that place?' Bilal cried.

'What you just saw is a prison with no walls, one of many started by Kali. They're everywhere and growing as we speak.'

'But how does Kali create these prisons?'

'People go into the prison of their own accord. They are tempted, not forced.'

'How?'

'They do it for gold. More and more gold, more wealth.'

'Are you saying wealth is a bad thing, sir?' asked Bilal. He had known what it was to be poor and had often wished he was richer.

'No Bilal. Wealth is not bad in itself. Imagine the good one can do with it. But what Kali has done is traded them wealth in exchange for their conscience. They have given up their judgement, their ability to decide what is right. Once people are without a conscience, they are at the mercy of their mind. All the mind can produce are selfish thoughts. So without a conscience to control them, people kill, maim, lie, steal, whatever they can, to get whatever it is they want.'

Bilal remembered again the horrors they had seen.

'But sir, they did not look happy; those people we saw,' he said.

'You're right, Bilal. They cannot be happy. Without a conscience, they lose the capacity for happiness. They run after the next mind-ruled idea, hoping that'll make them happy. So on and on they go, getting more and more caught up in Kali's world, more and more miserable, but worshipping no one else, giving Kali unlimited power. Kali becomes the only god to be worshipped, and humans destroy each other, trying to have more. Just like he wants.'

Bilal spoke up.

'How do we stop Kali?'

'It sounds ridiculously simple, but believe me that it's the only way: conscience over mind. The mind tells us what we want, but the conscience tells us what is right.'

'But the right thing for one person is not necessarily the right thing for another.'

'Killing, exploiting others, hurting another person in any way—these things can never be right. You know that without my telling you. Everyone does.

But yes, there are some rights and wrongs that are unique for each of us, and are governed by a voice in our heads that we call conscience. If we refuse to listen to that voice, the mind goes out of control and just wants more and more, with no regard to anyone or anything else. The uncontrolled mind is the doorway Kali uses to tempt people into his prisons.'

'And you? Were you ever tempted?'

His teacher looked into the distance for some time. Bilal wondered what his thoughts were.

Finally, he spoke, measuring each word.

'I was in the prison for the longest time, perhaps its longest serving inmate. But my temptation was not wealth; it was hatred of a caste. I was a mass murderer. I killed a clan—Kshatriyas if you must know—not once, but twenty-one times. I am probably one of the rare few who managed to set themselves free. I am Parashuram, and I have spent three yugs atoning for the things I did while I was trapped in there. There's still miles to go.'

He sighed deeply, as if saying this had relieved him of a very great load. Two tears appeared at the corner of each eye. Instinctively, Bilal knew he should look away. He looked down at the ground, giving Parashuram some time to recover from this uncharacteristic wave of emotion.

His guru finally smiled.

'So, Bilal miah, here we are, a handful of souls trying to free the largest prison camp that ever existed.'

'But where do I come in, sir? How can I rescue them?' Bilal felt helpless and scared in the face of the responsibility that seemed to be placed on him.

'You don't understand the power of your own compassion, Bilal,' said Parashuram. 'Perhaps you cannot do anything yet, but you needed to see it, so that when the time comes, you will know what is to be done.

'Vishnu's message for humanity was to look within its own conscience and use its intelligence, its creativity to find heaven on earth. People need to be stopped from this path they are on, one that will only lead to carnage. They need to be brought back to celebrate their conscience. That is when humans will know their true power. That is what your role as the avatar is.'

THE SECOND READING

In his private chamber, Kali found a little square of light flickering in front of his desk. A message. Sensing his presence, the square expanded to a screen that filled the far wall. Dambha and Nirritti were standing in the frame. Anrit was walking over to the group from a distance away. Nirritti looked grim; Dambha was smirking at her discomfiture.

'What is it, my children?' The Supremo was in a benevolent mood.

'Greetings, Supremo,' said Dambha in a silky voice, looking concerned and pleased at the same time, as if he knew something unpleasant that his boss did not. Nirritti was silently staring at the ground.

'Well, what's the matter?'

'I'm afraid we have bad news, Supremo. One of the village boys has disappeared. He left a week ago.'

'So? I thought you had got the Enemy.'

'Well, the circumstances need checking out, but the boy was apparently part of the magic play that was under scrutiny.'

'Nirritti?' The Supremo looked at her with cold questioning eyes.

She paled under his gaze. 'Supremo—I just heard of this from one of the actors.' She dragged a terrified-looking Madan by the hair into the frame. He was whimpering with fear.

Anrit spoke for the first time. 'This boy tells me that there was another in their troupe—a boy in charge of ... of special effects,' he stumbled before the last three words. 'This last boy has not been seen since the night of the play. It was a dry summer night, so no footsteps were visible on the hard ground. His parents have already been taken in. They claim to know nothing.'

'Supremo, if I might interrupt—sending just these two without any Council members was always underestimating the enemy,' Dambha cut in, eager to push his case for seniority. 'After all, their partial human lineage limits them and somewhat dilutes their powers. Perhaps the will to carry out the manhunt with the fullest energy can only belong to those who are truly from Vishasha?'

Nirritti looked at Dambha like she would pulverise him.

'You know perfectly well that Anrit is my half-brother; it's his mother who was human, not mine. Not that I would ever doubt his loyalty.'

Anrit kept his cool, although his frown betrayed his humiliation.

Kali looked at the brother and sister duo.

'Anrit, Nirritti, I'll give you another chance to prove yourselves. Dambha, should there be another failure, I'll ask you to take over. I'm sending Kokh and Vikokh there right away for analysis. Anrit, see if you can do something with the traces this boy has left behind. In the meantime, punish the whole village. Let the treatment be harsh—I'm not necessarily looking for survivors. I trust that at least this small job won't be difficult for an agent of your stature?' His voice was as cold as an icicle as he addressed Nirritti.

She bowed, and he waved the window shut with an irritated flick of the wrist.

He was not at peace. No amount of tossing and turning would help, so he got up and went to the Other Room. Kokh and Vikokh, those masters of illusion, had made it for him and no one in his city state knew of its existence, save the three of them.

It didn't have a key; it had to be summoned into existence from inside him.

Kali closed his eyes for a moment until the room appeared. Then opening his eyes, he turned the door handle and walked in.

The room felt viscous, like the inside of a person's body. It seemed as if it could expand or contract manifold; the walls were like human tissue and not solid. Kali walked further in.

He faced a set of moving images, like a film reel. He saw himself, born fully formed from his father's fear. His father had never been able to get over his awe of Nature or the fear of his existence ending at Nature's whim. Each of his offspring had been conceived with the desire to bring Nature to heel. Kali's weapon to that end had been greed and the vices.

Not that Kali had ever complained. The lure of all he provided had led people to act for material gain, instead of going by the dictates of their conscience. They had stopped caring whether their actions were morally right or wrong, provided they were materially right. All this had made him a supremely powerful god.

And now it was all going to end, if the prophecy was to be believed. This so-called messiah would take all his power away, bring him face to face with his own end—Kali shuddered at this—and let nature win over Earth. A god's death is not the same as a human's for, strictly speaking, he couldn't die, but he would be shut away, made powerless or blown away into particles finer than an atom and scattered all over the universe.

Everything he had built over the last four yugs would be destroyed, all his power and control taken away. He would lose all his influence, his wealth, his worshippers ... it would take him an eternity to come back to the strength he currently enjoyed.

Well, it would just have to be stopped. He would not give up an inch if he could help it. The avatar would have to be identified and eliminated. He and only he would be worshipped on Earth. And why not? It was the humans who had chosen to put material wealth above all others, at the cost of everything else that made life rich—he was just a catalyst.

He closed his eyes and went inside, deep within his consciousness, through masses of flesh and tissue. Finally, he reached a locked cabinet. Closing his eyes, he opened the door. The cabinet, empty at first, suddenly held a cloth sack. Reaching out with eager hands, Kali opened up the neck of the sack and poured out the contents on his palm. Five blood-red stones fell out, gleaming in the half-light. Kali clutched the stones in his palm. He must have all ten—the final guarantee of success against the Enemy.

Emerging from the Other Room, Kali switched on his screen. 'Get Dhoomvati,' he barked to his secretary. He needed an expert opinion.

She was not happy at this treatment. All gods have large egos and Dhoomavati was no exception. Her eyes flashed and her face was dark with anger. She banged her winnow on Kali's desk and snapped, 'Well?' Even Durukti flinched at the sight.

'I need you to do another reading for me,' said Kali, calmly.

'I may not be beyond the grip of all ego like the Supreme Mahesh or Vishnu, but I *am* a goddess. You don't drag me in like a common soothsayer every time you get the jitters, Kali.'

The Supremo's eyes flashed yellow and his tongue lolled out—a rare lapse, revealing his loss of mental control for a moment. He held his temper, however. The Seer was needed at this point.

'I apologise, Dhoomavati. But I needed to know something. I need to find a missing boy.'

She fished for a cigarette in her matted hair and lit it. 'Scared of death, after having acquired all this over the eons?'

'So should you be, Dhoomavati. You think the other gods want their stint to end?'

'What do you mean?' asked Dhoomavati sharply.

Kali responded, a shade too fast, 'They'll all be on my side when the time comes, you'll see.'

'Do not lie to me, Kali. I am the Great Void. I existed before this creation and I shall remain once creation ends. Your petty concerns do not affect me at all.' She threw some rice grains on her winnow and gave it a shake, then concentrated. The cigarette smouldered forgotten in one reedy hand.

The grains had made an axe.

'He has met the Bhriguputra and is under his tutelage now.'

'Parashuram? Where is he?'

She tossed the rice grains again, muttering a question under her breath, but this time the grains fell at random. Then, of their own volition, they rearranged themselves in the shape of a plough. Dhoomavati shook her head, mystified.

'Very strange. The rice grains won't tell me. But I'll tell you what—they keep forming the plough.'

Barely concealing his irritation, Kali said, 'Plough?'

'Balram's sign. There is a Balram for every Krishna, a staunch ally, a brother in arms. This means two things—your quarry is definitely the saviour and his key is Balram. Find Balram and he'll guide you to the messiah.'

'Where is this Balram now?'

Dhoomavati gave the winnow another shake. This time the letters fell in the shape of the Devnagri letter 'A', then rearranged to make three horizontal lines.

'The devotee of Shiva with a name starting with 'A'—that would be Ashwatthama. He is, or is going to be, with Ashwatthama.'

Kali tapped his desk—a strange expression on his face. 'Isn't it foresaid that the only human who can recognise the avatar is Ashwatthama?'

Dhoomavati snapped her fingers in excitement. 'Of course! That's what is meant to happen! Everyone holds a piece of the puzzle, but no one has the complete information. Ashwatthama can recognise, but not find, the avatar, and Balram can find, but not recognise him.'

'Balram—' Kali tapped his desk again, a strange expression on his face. Then, changing his tone, 'Tell me about Dambha. I need an assessment.'

She looked again. A trumpet. 'All too often, he is a victim of his own weapon, the bluster. Devious, untrustworthy. Be careful, he can be seduced with promises of power.'

Kali's eyes were hooded, his expression hidden from her.

As she disappeared, Dhoomavati couldn't help feeling he knew something she didn't.

A TRAP IS SET

Kokh and Vikokh swooped over the village, flying down with Anrit and Nirritti. All four of them were dressed as army officers.

'The official story is that the army needs to check the area for terrorists. The villagers have been told to cooperate,' explained Anrit, in his current form as a major in the Indian army.

'We'll start with the backstage area, then move to the missing boy's home, then all his haunts in this village. Have you got his friend?' asked General Kokh.

'Nirritti's fetching him. Meanwhile, let's go ahead.'

The stage was deserted. A month's dust had gathered undisturbed on everything.

No one had come here since the day of the play. Backstage was mostly pigeon shit and rubble. The odd prop from different shows had been left behind, but which were from the magic play?

'You can ask him,' said Nirritti, shoving a shivering Madan towards the three of them.

Madan looked terrified. He had become almost half his earlier size; his cheeks were sunken, his eyes glazed. Gone was the cheerful boy who burst into song at the slightest pretext. He seemed to be in a trance, but even in this state he sensed the terrifying power of the four in front of him, for he whimpered to himself as he stood.

Kokh snapped a finger and Madan's eyes focussed, taking in the present. He cowered before them.

'We need your help, boy, to find out something about this friend of yours,' said the General.

'Bilal? I haven't seen him since that … that night,' said Madan, passing his tongue over parched lips.

'We know. We just need a sample of the props he made for your play, boy. Are any of them lying around? There's a reward in it for you.'

Madan started his search, crawling on all fours and peering under old furniture, opening up the costume cupboard and looking through the bric-a-brac. When he finished, he had found two things—a 'gold' coin and a piece of rock from the sim-sim cave doors. Vikokh took them from him with his forceps and stored them carefully in envelopes, as always.

'Will you let me go, then?' asked Madan, a desperate edge to his voice.

Nirritti, leading Madan away, said silkily, 'All in good time. We still need you for a while.' They could hear the boy's hysterical begging and sobbing as he was being led back to the prison.

That evening, after General Kokh's customary Security Council meeting (now held every week), Anrit and the twins sat evaluating the clues in Kokh-Vikokh's chamber.

As the general placed the coin on an instrument that looked like a microscope, Vikokh explained, 'As I calibrate this, you should be able to see the last time this coin was handled. Only for a few minutes, but it should help.'

The coin lay still on the instrument for a few seconds, then a fine vibration went through it. In front of the three of them, a rectangular window opened up. The play was in progress. Madan was playing Ali Baba, holding up the coins and laughing in delight. The curtains fell to thunderous applause, a bit muffled due to the passage of time.

His twin clutched Vikokh's shoulder. 'Just before the curtains closed, just slow down there.'

As the film slowed down to half its speed, then a quarter, the trio saw an arm in a checked full-sleeved shirt, waving at the pots of gold.

'Quick, the other clue!'

Vikokh put the rock from the cave on the instrument this time, his fingers quivering with excitement. This time, there was a little more than an arm, they could make out a bit of the form as well. The boy had extraordinarily fair hands.

The General paused the film. 'Mind games and deception are your forte, Anrit. Can you do it?' he asked.

'It's a long shot, without the face, but I'll try,' said the agent. Holding the rock in an iron grip, he closed his eyes. The others saw a cloud screen the little image window in front, before extinguishing it altogether.

'The trap is laid, but whether he bites the bait and reveals himself to us is up to him,' said Anrit.

'How?' asked Vikokh.

Anrit shrugged. 'Does he know the difference between mind and conscience?'

PRIVATE CONVERSATIONS

Bilal walked away from his teacher, thinking hard. He was upset and confused. A lot of the things his teacher disapproved of, were fun. It was fun to be the centre of attention, fun to be rich, to buy things, to look good, to eat well. These things by themselves wouldn't make me a bad person, he thought. Being rich didn't make a person good or bad. Plenty of poor people were unkind and there were enough prosperous people who did good. Judging was so complicated.

He wished he was back in his village, playing cricket with his friends. Life was so much simpler then. He swallowed hard and blinked back his tears. It was too much for a boy like him. The pressure to just survive was intense and relentless and he was only fourteen. Plenty of boys his age or older had nothing to worry about.

'Right you are.'

'Who's that?'

'Who do you think?'

'There's no one here.'

'Then I must be invisible.'

Bilal looked all around him. Still nothing.

'You've searched the outside. What about the inside?'

'You mean … you're in me?'

'I am your soul, Bilal.'

'You're joking! Souls don't speak.'

'Look, I'll prove it to you. I'll tell you what you were thinking of right now. You were wishing you were back in your village, playing cricket with the boys.'

Bilal was silent. The voice had got it right. He looked around. No one else seemed to have seen or heard anything. So it was speaking from inside him, as it had claimed. It felt strange to talk to his own soul.

'If you miss your home so much, perhaps you need to say goodbye one last time before you leave. Your parents must be worried.'

'I can't go. Bhargav Sir has forbidden me to leave. He feels it's unsafe.'

'Are you sure you can trust him?'

'What do you mean? He's my teacher!'

'He's also a mass murderer, isn't he? To decimate a community twenty-one times, what kind of a person does that?'

Bilal kept quiet. The voice had made a powerful point.

'How do you know he isn't using you in the name of this—this misadventure to wipe out the Kshatriyas a twenty-second time?'

'Be quiet! My head's bursting.'

'As you wish, Bilal. I'm always here for you.' The voice fell silent.

Bilal wished his soul was back, almost immediately. He had never felt this lonely before.

He was sitting with Parashuram on the parapet of his tiny cottage. Bilal had considered asking his teacher about his recent experience, in the life skills class. It seemed strange, somehow, to have extended conversations with an independent entity inside his head, so he decided to discuss it in confidence with Bhargav. But he couldn't just blurt it out. Being able to hear one's soul sounded abnormal, almost crazy. So he discussed his other questions while he mustered up the courage to mention it.

Parashuram didn't believe in idle conversation, so they shelled peas while they talked. Bilal spoke about this and that while he wondered how to get to the point.

'Look son, why don't you ask me what you've come to ask? You're not paying attention to what I'm saying.' Bilal had absentmindedly put the peas where the pods went.

Bilal gulped, took a deep breath and blurted out about the voice claiming to be his soul. Better out than in.

'As long as it rings true, listen to your voice,' said his teacher. 'But remember that there's a difference between our mind and our soul. Our mind sometimes plays tricks on us. Mine convinced me that wiping out the Kshatriyas was the right thing to do. Not once, but twenty-one times. It was a gateway to the prison, but I couldn't tell.'

'But this felt different, more friendly. It didn't say anything unpleasant.' Bilal omitted what was actually said, however, fearing a reaction from his teacher.

'Use your moral core, your conscience, to judge. Listen very carefully to the voice before you take any action. Every impulse is not necessarily correct. And remember, our soul doesn't always sound pleasant and polite and kind. It can say some harsh things. It's meant to.'

Bilal thanked his teacher and left, thinking hard. Parashuram sat looking at him after he left, a frown creasing his forehead.

Anrit took a deep breath to steady his nerves before he started. Deception was a tightrope walk; one misstep and he could be dead. Reprisals on Vishasha were swift and violent. Only perfection guaranteed his survival. A few more deep breaths and his fear subsided somewhat. Now for the task at hand.

Bilal walked deep into the jungle in search of firewood. At least, that was his pretext for spending some time alone. It had been a week since he had had the chat with his teacher. His soul had been talking to him every day since.

'Why do you not contact your parents if you can appear and disappear at will?'

'I told you—Bhargav Sir thinks it's a bad idea.'

'And you? What do you think?'

Bilal shrugged. He missed his parents very much.

'Whom do you miss most—your mother or father?'

'My mother,' said Bilal unhesitatingly.

'Well, don't you think you should go and meet her once—just to tell her you're safe?'

'Look, I told you, Sir thinks it's highly dangerous, all right?'

'What? He thinks your enemies are lying in wait at the village? And what does your judgement tell you? Do you have any or not?'

Bilal kept quiet at this barb.

'Suit yourself, then. But if you're really as powerful as Bhargav Sir says you are, it shouldn't be a problem. I just expected you to be your own man, that's all.'

Bilal hacked away at a dead log lying at his feet. The camp rules forbade them from cutting live branches. A family of termites ran helter-skelter into the undergrowth. He hoped he hadn't killed any.

His soul was correct in a way. It was only fair to meet his mother once and to say goodbye. No one need know. He could disappear tonight and be back before anyone knew.

He could do it now.

'You'll be back before you know it,' said his new friend.

Anrit, Nirritti, Dambha and the Third Gender Force waited patiently inside the hut. Vyadhi, Jara, Shoke, Trishna and Krodhe were Kali's force of choice when it came to armed manoeuvres of any kind. They had been pulled out of their last mission—that of subjugating Japan—in order to guard the trap.

Thanks to Anrit's sorcery, the team could hear the conversation between Bilal and his false soul. For it was indeed the voice that Anrit had sent out on that day using the memory from the rock. All they could do was listen, however. There was no way to control or manipulate the magic as there was so little of the physical entity to go upon.

In the last ten days since the trap had been set, the wait had been agonising. They had come frustratingly close to their objective, but the fish hadn't bitten. Twice, the boy had betrayed a strong wish to visit his village, held back only by the order given to him by his guru. It was frustrating, especially with Dambha snapping at their heels, eager to take advantage. Nirritti had assumed Rukhsana's form in anticipation of his visit each time, only to return to her true self a day later. But today was different.

They heard out the last conversation in silence. Nirritti changed as fast as she could, motioning to the others to stay hidden inside the hut. In what seemed like the flash of an eye, Bilal landed with a soft thud on the threshold of his hut, the axe with which he was chopping wood still in his hand. Nirritti stepped out with tearful eyes, the picture of motherly love.

'Bilal! I thought I'd never see you again! Where, oh, where have you been?' She held out her arms to him.

Bilal rushed into his mother's arms, as she held him tightly in a hug … a hug which swiftly turned into a vice-like grip on his arms. Puzzled, he looked into her eyes.

'You stupid, *stupid* boy,' mocked the voice inside his head.

Suddenly it was all a whirl. At the same instant when Bilal wielded his axe to fend off the surrounding five demons, his teacher landed in a cloud of dust, his axe in one hand.

'Hang in there, boy!' said his familiar voice as he hacked off the arms of three of the force— Shoke, Jara and Trishna—in one mighty blow. Then, grabbing Bilal by the collar, he hacked Dambha into two with his axe, jumped up high, and vanished into nothingness in front of Nirritti's disbelieving eyes.

'Explain yourself,' he panted, as he threw Bilal on to the ground once they reached camp. 'Did I not forbid you to return to the village? This is exactly the sort of trick I was afraid of. What possessed you?'

Bilal, shamefaced, told him everything.

'It wasn't your soul you were listening to, Bilal,' said his teacher emphatically. 'What you heard was your mind, playing tricks on you, like mine did. The little twinge of doubt, the tiny bit of guilt at disobeying advice designed to protect you, that was your conscience speaking. If you don't listen to what your conscience tells you, you'll never hear your soul's directives. Your gifts are not meant to be used for instant gratification, Bilal.

'I suspected this the other day when you spoke to me. I've had the benefit of experience, after all. I saw you withdrawing into yourself for long hours, neglecting your training, staring at nothing in particular while you dreamed the hours away, classic signs of being lured in. Then, the warning came. So I followed you into the jungle.'

'You were warned? By whom?'

'The identity was kept a secret from us. But someone, at great risk to his or her own self, warned us about a trap being laid for you. I was alert for any changes in your behaviour.'

Bilal hung his head. He was miserable. There was a camp full of people risking their lives for him, and he had decided to risk it all for his personal sentiment. He could barely look at his teacher.

'Chin up, Bilal,' he said kindly, no longer angry. Parashuram was as quick to calm down as he was to rouse. 'The good thing is that you now know what it feels like to be tempted, otherwise all your knowledge would have been theoretical. Just live in the present, lead an active life, without dreaming about the past or the future, and you'll know you're safe from harm.

'And this present moment tells me that it's time for dinner. And I'm very hungry. Aren't you?' asked his teacher, smiling.

Bilal smiled back. At the moment, he was very thankful for the present.

The lake was gigantic, still and dark. It was as if its depths could swallow anything and everything. Nothing lived in it. They said it was cursed, but scientists reasoned that it was the salt water of the lake that gave that impression. That night, it seemed forbidding. There was no moon. The lonely snow-clad landscape was lit scantily by stars.

On the banks of the lake, two silhouettes were huddled in close conversation. One of them was enormous, and overshadowed the other, who, though he was gigantic by normal standards, seemed nondescript in comparison. A putrid smell filled the air.

Snatches of speech floated through the silence. 'The guide ... the weapon ... the wordkeeper suspects ... according to plan ... start from Burhanpur ... use the guide ...'

The enormous shadow stood up, his curly mane glinting in the moonlight. Wrapping a shawl around himself to hide his face, he stepped away from the lake and followed the path into the mountains. The stench reduced somewhat.

At the lake, the other man sat, deep in thought.

ANYA'S NEW LIFE

Anya and the Chiranjeevi trekked eastward where the jungle was deeper. He had flatly refused to talk while they were still amongst people. Up close, he was even larger than Anya had dreamt. His clothes hung loosely on his frame and most of his visible limbs were covered in oozing bandages. Only the wound on his forehead was open, a gaping black hole that gave her the shivers every time she looked at it. Anya averted her eyes, realising that the Chiranjeevi had seen her shudder of revulsion.

'You can go ahead and look, I'm used to it by now. When I don't want anyone to stare at me, I simply make myself unseen.'

'How do you do that?'

'If you are still and uninteresting for long enough, you will find that you are invisible as far as the world is concerned. Someday I shall show you how. You need to rest first.'

They had reached a thicket of trees in the middle

of the jungle. Anya could tell that no one ever came here. The place looked haunted, for one thing. An eerie blue mist hung over it in the early morning light. There were no signs of life, no birds, no animals, just a stillness, an uneasy peace. They walked straight on.

It was darker inside the thicket than in the jungle outside. Tall tropical trees stopped the sunlight from penetrating anywhere below the first few feet. The mist added a greyish tinge to everything. Unlike the sunlight, it seemed to seep down to eye level, obscuring her vision. She could barely see five feet in front of her. Her companion had disappeared ahead but his voice was guiding her steps.

'You will need to walk on straight for three hundred yards. Watch your step; don't trip on the roots. There is a clearing out there, with a deserted temple.'

She walked on, not wondering any longer, just happy to reach a destination of some kind. When the jungle cleared, she found a field with vegetable patches, a couple of fruit trees and an ancient temple. And strangely enough, a cable TV wire.

'Welcome to my home, wordkeeper. I have been living here for the past two hundred years.' The voice spoke behind her.

Anya turned round to find the giant from her dreams leaning against a sal tree.

'Hullo Anya', he said again. 'You may call me Rakshak. The locals do.' To Anya's relief, he didn't bother to shake her hand. It was wrapped in filthy oozing bandages and two of the fingers were reduced to stumps.

Anya had now spent a week in the jungle, and three nights at her new base. The Chiranjeevi had arranged for her to sleep inside the temple while he slept under the open sky. Apparently, this was out of preference. Anya was gradually learning not to stare at the terrible wound on his forehead.

The Chiranjeevi had been training her for survival in the jungle. They would start early in the morning when he made her run. Anya had never been very active and half a mile was all she could manage the first day. She had tearfully asked to be let off. He'd shaken his head and said she would need to be able to run eight miles every day by the end of the training.

Anya knew better than to argue in the middle of a jungle, but she just couldn't see how she would achieve that. Her camp activities had progressed better. She had learnt how to make a fire from sticks, just in case she could never emerge into civilisation again. Tending the vegetable patch was even easier. Anya had her mother's green fingers. She had even tried her hand at cooking the previous night. The Chiranjeevi had grains and pulses stocked inside the temple, and she discovered she wasn't bad at survival cooking.

'How did you get the rice and dal? Didn't anyone see you?' she asked him, gulping down the food greedily after the long day.

He smiled, his teeth gleaming in the dark. 'It's my salary.'

'But, you're top secret ... your existence, I mean,' she blurted out.

'There have always been people in this part of the world who have known of me. One day, a couple of hundred years ago, I got a strange letter from the local tehsildar. He'd left it pinned to a tree near the temple. He said that he knew I lived here, and although he didn't want to meddle with my life, he had to enlist my help. The forests were about to change, now that the British would be ruling over India, he said. The poor man had been appointed Forest Ranger in these parts and he was terrified of annoying me, in case I tore him from limb to limb or cursed him with leprosy ... you know how people fear the unknown. And he couldn't say no to his British masters, either. So I wrote back, asking him what the job involved.

'It was nothing short of being in charge of the jungles out here. Management of forests, the game—

for the British were big game hunters—and the judicious clearing of patches where the army would wish to station its troops. My last refuge was to be overrun by people. Who knows, perhaps the British would wish to capture and parade me as some sort of a freak in circuses? I was desperate to retain my little bit of jungle here.

'Then an idea struck me. I wrote back to the tehsildar, suggesting that I would take over his job. I would be the Ranger on the ground, and he could keep the job on paper. This would give me the opportunity to shape the jungles near Burhanpur as I wished. I could stay hidden forever that way. I just wanted to be paid in pulses and cereal. He did one better. He actually got me employed—so I periodically made reports to my superiors who would nervously look for the voice that spoke to them. My official name became Rakshak. When the Indian government came to power, the locals maintained the same system, although I am no longer the officially appointed Ranger here. But the man drawing my salary knows the rules.'

'So you know these jungles well.'

'I made these jungles what they are today. Every inch of it has been planned by me, Anya.'

'Didn't you ever, ever feel like asking for something else besides the grains?'

'Well, I did get the television, and the radio before that. News, especially offbeat, strange news is important for my survival.'

'So that's why you have cable?'

Rakshak smiled his grim smile.

Anya thought about her strange guardian as she went inside the temple that night. He needs some new bandages, she thought.

Anya was dreaming of feet. She saw herself on a swing, pushing herself higher and higher with her bare feet, while her mother looked on. Ma had rubber slippers on her feet and was working in her garden. Anya swung higher and higher, until the garden seemed like a tiny square patch beneath her. As she swung back towards the ground, her mother came closer. She was smiling and pointing at her feet. Anya looked at them. They were fine, except the second toes were taller than the first.

Then she turned into half-bird, half-Ma, and flew away. Anya flew with her, over brown earth and muddy plains, until she reached a green hill—a forested hill. Ma beckoned to her as she swooped down, Anya following close behind. They came closer and closer to the blue-green tropical forest, piercing through its deep canopy until they were on top of a sea of tents. In the middle stood a man, dressed in army fatigues, but with ash stripes on his forehead. Anya tried, but couldn't see his face clearly. Ma pointed at him and as Anya looked from her to the camp and back to her, her face changed to that of the yaksha. He mouthed 'shhh' and flew up into the sky.

Another week passed. Anya was getting better at running, now that the initial aches and pains had subsided. Rakshak was teaching her how to use a knife as a weapon in close combat. Anya had her own little fruit knife to practice with. She had learnt to feint and to thrust her knife in, but that was about it. Her time was mostly spent practising Rakshak's specified movements in the air or at attacking fixed targets held up by him.

'Show some aggression, Anya, you must develop a little more courage. No, no, don't step back, you'll put yourself in a corner that way. Attack instead. There are escape routes in front of you.' Anya sighed and put her knife down.

'We've been at it for hours, Rakshak. Can we stop now? I just can't think any more.'

'You've got to build up your stamina. Tiredness is what your opponent will be waiting for. When we're tired, we make mistakes. When we're afraid, we're passive. Neither is desirable in a fight.'

Anya nodded dully. She couldn't think any further. Rakshak left her alone—he knew he'd pushed her a lot that day. As she curled up on the mattress that night, Anya wondered where her mother was.

She slept badly that night. Every time she dozed off, the ceiling seemed to develop a tear through which she glimpsed a face. After her fourth failed attempt at sleeping, Anya stepped outside.

Rakshak was sitting, leaning against a tree, with his eyes on the night sky. He motioned her to come and sit next to him.

'Who are you?' she asked abruptly. 'I mean, who are you actually?'

Rakshak looked at her with hooded eyes for a while before he spoke. 'A long, long time ago, I was Ashwatthama, the cursed immortal from the Mahabharat. The only person in eternity for whom living forever is not a boon, but a curse. And yes, it is a fate worse than death.'

For the rest of the night, Anya heard Ashwatthama's story.

DHOOMAVATI'S DECISION

Dhoomavati took a long drag on the cigarette and exhaled. The smoke left her nostrils in two serpentine coils, making her look like a dragon. Curse this permanent hunger. No amount of food, alcohol and tobacco could quell her unending appetite. Hungry, forever hungry, irrespective of how much she ate or drank. Why am I a goddess, she thought bitterly. This never-ending hunger is a miserable curse I bear through all eternity.

She looked around her. Her crematorium. Others may come and go, but for her, this was home. Miles of scorched ground, burnt remains of cremations and her collection of skulls over eons of being here. No one came to this end, except the odd soul who wanted her brand of salvation: extreme solitude. Rarely worshipped in this form, she was the recipient of the strangest gifts—all manner of food, sacred or otherwise, alcohol, cigarettes. It was a taboo existence, this, but it gave her a deep insight into the end of an era.

Dhoomavati sighed. For all her bravado, she did not understand Mahesh's Grand Design. What possible use was she to creation in this form? A goddess of loneliness, with an unending appetite and the added curse of seeing the future (for which she got harassed by a constant stream of annoying people both human and divine), she was banished to crematoriums and the altars of widows. The trickle of disengaged souls who insisted on worshipping her with cigarettes was hardly a consolation. Didn't they know she would have to have whatever they gave her? Why did humans understand everything so literally?

She took a second drag and watched the smoke serpents coil away into the moonless night. Her stomach rumbled painfully, but she concentrated on the task at hand. There would be time enough to experience pangs of hunger.

The rice grains were more important. They were refusing to speak to her about the avatar, something she had not experienced in thousands of years. Perhaps she needed to alter the question.

Thinking of a related question, she took the winnow in her hand and gave it another light shake. The rice grains and some tiny black gravel leapt up in the air, then settled on the winnow. Not bothering to remove the gravel, Dhoomavati concentrated instead on the pattern the grains made. They had separated into two broad shapes: one in the shape of the Devnagri letter 'ba' and the other showing the outline of a mountain with a castle of some sort.

So there was a Balram. She knew that already.

Dhoomavati gave the winnow another shake. The grains rose and fell again, making a familiar sign of a circle with a cross under it. Dhoomavati crowed with laughter, rocking on her haunches.

A girl! Balram is a girl?

The rice grains reiterated their message, arranging themselves again to show the mountain range with a castle on top. Or was it a fort? There were some ridges on the mountain that looked like ramparts. It was a fort.

Asirgarh. This could only mean one thing: the time had come.

Her last discussion with Kali had worried her a great deal. There was something he had been hinting at: 'You think the other gods want their stint to end?' Who could he have been talking about? Brahma, Vishnu, Mahesh and she were the eternal four, although everyone knew that they would change forms and moods over time. She herself would morph several times over, from the void form of Dhoomavati at the end of this kalpa to nurturing Kamala, by the time the next one had got into stride. As the times changed, so would she, and so would the Trinity.

But yes, the lesser gods, though immortal, would not continue forever. Godhood was essentially a designation, albeit an unimaginably long one when measured in human years. When this kalpa ended, they would face the new one with different roles and responsibilities. An uncertain time, to say the least.

She tossed the rice grains in her winnow and asked which gods might be supporting Kali. Unsurprisingly, the grains remained scattered. Most gods had the power to block direct questions like this. She would have to do better. That is, if there was anything there at all. She asked again, a more general question this time, 'What is Kali's aim for the Earth?'

The rice grains fell on the winnow at random again, but this time, they were of pure gold. That figures, thought Dhoomavati. The Earth is full of gold, humans having barely scratched the surface of the crust in their quest for the yellow metal. She set the winnow aside and fished out another cigarette from her matted hair.

The grains kept moving, however. From the corner of her left eye, she saw them form the shape of a serpent, then lie still. She turned around, mesmerised. The rice grain serpent was now growing another head, this time at the other end. Then, in front of her, the serpent twisted on itself, pulling and stretching in two opposite directions in a churning motion, until it snapped apart and scattered across the winnow.

She threw her cigarette away and raced to the winnow, giving it another shake, mouthing silent question after silent question, but the grains remained stubbornly still.

Dhoomavati lit another cigarette, taking no notice of her pet crow who perched on her skeletal shoulder.

A manthan—a great churning. Manthans always spelt destruction on a gigantic scale and for a long stretch of time, a thing that directly conflicted with her mandate of watchful protection over the cosmos.

Kali had finally over-reached. It was time to choose her loyalties. Besides, she wanted to see the prophecy unfold with her own eyes. She stubbed out her cigarette with an impatient gesture.

'We're off on a journey, Karkash. Get prepared to travel from place to place.'

The crow jumped off her shoulder and groomed his feathers. Finishing off a smattering of human brain that he'd been saving for later, he folded his wings together and started to grow. By the time Dhoomavati emerged from her hut with her winnow, broom, rice grains and cigarettes, he was the size of a small car. Wordlessly, she mounted him.

With a steady whoosh-whoosh, Karkash flapped his wings, pulling his feet up.

They disappeared into the night sky, Dhoomavati's crazy hair the only white thing in the pitch-black darkness.

PART THREE

PART THREE

Notes from an Immortal

I, Vibhishan, past Lord of the Sinhala land of Lanka, immortal by the grace of my Lord Ram, and the general of the wordkeepers, write the following.

Garud tells me that the Seer can no longer be found. She and her mount flew off into the darkness one night. Two beggars came looking for her soon after. Since no one other than myself and Kali's agents know of her existence, it is safe to assume she's chosen her allegiance and has gone to join whichever side she has picked in her usual whimsical manner.

But why? Is she showing signs of having a conscience, finally? Is she coming to us? And if so, *can she be trusted?*

TANYA

It was the night of the now weekly Security Council dinner. Members were relaxing with wine and cognac after a particularly long strategy session. But the Supremo had other postprandial plans. Shunning his usual bodyguards, he walked from the Security Council's office towards less hallowed parts of his facility, taking Durukti and Shoke with him. Doors opened automatically with a touch of his index finger. The ground seemed to tilt upwards with every step, until they were very close to the surface.

They could hear the dust storm in the distance, the first one this week. The Supremo touched the last door with his index finger, and climbed the sloping path. He could always fly up, but he liked to prolong the experience as much as he could. All this was his domain; around him were living proof of the outcome for those who had dared to step out of line and defy his way. He liked to remind them that he had won after all. Where was Vishnu now?

They were at the base of the West Tower, which stretched over many storeys; sloping pathways seemed to disappear into the horizon when one looked up. The first two floors of the tower were administrative in nature, consisting of offices, dormitories and kitchens. The prisons started after that. The lower floors used conventional methods—torture and brutalisation—both useful in the extraction of information from ordinary prisoners. The upper floors were meant for people who had successfully resisted the earlier treatment. More refined methods were called for here. Hence Durukti and Shoke.

They walked right up to the top floor. An ordinary mortal would have had to rest in between. The din of the dust storm was terrible here. Red boulders were flying across the planet, smashing into anything above the surface and into each other. The air was thick with brick red dust. It was difficult to hear anything, difficult to breathe, difficult even to think with the noise.

The topmost cell had no guard. It was the most solitary of solitary confinements, there was no one even to watch over the cell.

He touched the door with his index finger, this time scratching it a little. The door swung open. Shutting the door behind him, Kali turned to face his prisoner. Durukti and Shoke stood behind. Their job was to observe the prisoner's behaviour and to delve into her thoughts for her deepest fears. They would begin when their master had finished.

She sat with her back to the door in a huddled mass. She looked old, about a hundred years. Her body had broken under torture, but his agents had not been able to make any headway into her mind. Somehow, something had kept her going through the pain. It was time to try another approach.

'I have come to tell you that you're a very brave woman, Tanya. Foolish, but brave.' She ignored him. Unperturbed, he continued, 'So I've come to make a deal with you. Tell me where the avatar is and I'll let your daughter be. She is only a teenager. This is not about her at all. All I need is the avatar and the other wordkeepers.'

There was no answer. He tried again.

'I shall spare her if you cooperate.'

Still nothing. Was she dead? Kali stepped closer, reaching out to check.

Tanya moved for the first time, shuddering at the touch. Her wounds had healed, but her smile was still bitter. 'Anya can look after herself, Kali. I've brought her up to be brave and independent. She has been trained to survive without her mother. I've lived with this possibility for enough time to plan for it.' And I—I've trained myself to be without her, she added in her thoughts.

'Aah, but you've never really been tested on that belief until now! Come, come—give me the avatar and I shall make you and your daughter richer than you can imagine. If you can throw in the amulets, I shall make you powerful as well. You will be able to influence the lives of millions. You can take your pick of prime positions. How do you think Rajanipati became prime minister?'

'The Prime Minister has changed?' asked Tanya, surprised.

'Deposed. In a coup. Along with most of his cabinet. Funny, no one has seen them since that day,' said Kali in a light voice.

Tanya forced herself to overcome her fear and look straight at him. 'Strange, I always thought it was the job of humans to bribe gods and not the other way round.'

'No? There's always a price for everyone, I find. The question is, what is yours? You give me what I want, I'll give you what you want.'

'Clearly, you have everything. What could a god possibly want from a human?'

Kali's face clouded over in frustration. The telltale tongue lolled out for a moment before it was swiftly pulled inside. He was angry, but still in control. He spat the words out.

'I want to decimate any challenge to my path. I want uncontrolled power over Earth. I want to be the only god to be worshipped and respected and feared. I rule gold, wine, the vices, power. I want these to be people's primary motivations. I have won over large swathes of the world's population who obediently serve me for these aims. But there are still a handful, like you, who can't be tamed. They still go on about the good of all, humanity and the good old gods. Bah! Humanity is happy to kill itself over the gifts I promise them. I would have killed you all too, except, your death doesn't give me power. It's when you live by my rules and worship me, all of you, that I become the Supreme God. And I will brook no challenges on my path for that.'

Keeping her voice carefully steady, Tanya said, 'You seem to be doing quite well on your own, then. Good luck.' Then she turned her back on him.

'Listen and listen carefully, wordkeeper. Sooner or later, I will find out what you fear the most. And I will make it come true, until you come begging to me for mercy, with your amulet and your daughter in tow. She escaped my attack within an inch of her life. But there is no escape for her on Earth. I have eyes and ears everywhere. She will be found, she will be killed, she will be made an example of!

'Your daughter's dead the next time I see her. And I promise you that it will be horrific.' He spun on his heel and left with Durukti following, waving the prison door shut with a flick of his wrist. Shoke stayed behind.

Tanya looked up and turned around once he was gone. Her heart felt cold and defeated. Her worst fear had already come true. Shoke looked deep into her eyes. Images of Anya flashed past—Anya hurt, injured, brutally tortured, cold ... a cry escaped her stubbornly shut mouth. Stop. Stop now. You know they haven't found her yet.

'It's the future that you see, prisoner,' was all Shoke said.

Liar. Remember, that's not happened yet, otherwise they wouldn't be here. She was finding it difficult to hold out against the deluge of terrible images. Think, Tanya, think. Something tranquil. Tranquil and beautiful. A faint picture loomed up through the mass of horrific ones. A beautiful garden with tall trees and long, undulating grasses, gently blowing through the breeze. Her garden. Yes, that's it. Keep trying.

Shoke took another deep breath and concentrated. Round two.

Tanya held on to her image, adding an imaginary palash tree to it. Its bare branches bore flowers, red flowers, blood red, they were made of blood. She whimpered.

Shoke smiled a thin smile and concentrated again. Round three.

Tanya was nearly fainting. Then in her delirium, she saw him, his handsome face with its lace collar. He was holding her hand, smiling gently.

Her one true love. She smiled.

The red storm raged on outside.

THE NEW
WORDKEEPER

General Kokh and his aide had not been seen in Vishasha for a while. The Council had to make do with the General's telepathic directions, transmitted from unknown locations. If they privately wondered what urgent matters made the General do ground visits, they kept their thoughts to themselves. It was not the Council's way to question the General.

They would have been surprised had they come across Kokh and Vikokh. Gone were the smart military uniforms. The duo was dressed in rags, sitting amongst a row of beggars at Sealdah station, while they discussed their next move. When on Earth, they preferred telepathic communication to actual words, an effective way to counter spying. Humans were so limited by their bodies.

'Are you sure we'll find her here?'

'This is Dhoomavati's favourite city. And

Keoratola her backyard. She won't leave Kolkata if she can help it.'

'It is essential that we go to the site she was picked up from. The clue won't talk otherwise.'

'We'll make our way there soon enough, after we've discussed our plan. No point in proceeding helter-skelter only to be outwitted.'

'We rush in, we ambush her and her crow, test the information on the site and bring her back. Simple and effective. We just have to remember to stick together, as always.'

They got up, the younger brother supporting the older sightless one, whose eyes were covered with dark glasses. As they walked on, they seemed to melt into the distance, which is exactly what they did. Kolkatans hurried past them, not noticing anything different. It was rush hour.

They re-emerged at dusk. Keoratola was thick with fumes from the traffic and the crematorium. It seemed impossible that there could be any place where the noise of the city couldn't reach. The two of them walked on southwards.

They had to cross the halfway point before the noise died down. Ahead, facing south, was a hut, which looked like it had been coated with dirty snow. Dhoomavati's crow had obviously made his own attempt at whitewashing his home.

'There's no one here—no signs of occupation either.'

An expletive reached Vikokh's mind. His brother was not happy.

'Check—check for clues. We need to know more right now. She's crucial to us, Vikokh. Our war plans need her Sight,' he added.

Vikokh didn't reply. Taking an envelope out of his cloth bundle, he emptied its contents on his palm—a burnt cigarette stub. The instrument in their office had yielded nothing. But sometimes, it helped to bring the object to the precise place where it had been used.

'Where exactly did we pick her up from that day? The day the Supremo brought her to us?'

'A little to the left—yes, yes, that's the neem tree. She was sitting and smoking under it.'

Moving closer to the tree, Vikokh touched the mouth end of the stub to the ground. For a while, nothing happened, then as the darkness gathered round them in that lonely spot, a faint image flickered in the space in front of him like an old film reel.

There was a man sitting in front of Dhoomavati. He seemed sixty-odd years old. His dark complexion and drooping white moustache made a striking contrast. Even in that dirty cemetery, he was wearing a natty three-piece suit and a tie. He seemed to be consulting Dhoomavati about something. A yellow parchment lay between them.

'The clue's too old for any kind of sound.'

'Shhh—keep watching.'

The man with the white moustache finished his conversation and turned to leave. As he rose from the floor with some discomfort, something glinted and was gone in a flash. Then the image disappeared.

'That last bit again, Vikokh. Make it slower this time.'

The twins watched very carefully the second time round, as the man turned.

Glinting on his tie was a simple silver tiepin, set with a red stone. It gleamed tantalisingly at them in the moonlight.

'Quick. Get the man's face out on all security channels on Earth and Vishasha. Ask them to be on standby,' said General Kokh. 'We have another wordkeeper.' And then to himself, 'That's it! That's what the bitch was hiding.'

Major Bhay of the Third Gender Force was waiting in the antechamber outside the General's room. It was a generally accepted fact that the Third Gender made the most committed soldiers as they felt no bond towards anyone except their own kind. Family was to them merely a vehicle for creation. Their nurture was Vishasha and the Supremo's responsibility. They hung out with other Third Gender folk and their commitment to work was exemplary.

Bhay was seen as a prominent candidate for the next round of promotions at Vishasha. Of course, he didn't mind the accolades that came his way. But that wasn't really why he did his job. It was the sheer joy of creating fear in the minds of others, the way it felt to be feared, the way fear smelled on others. He was addicted to it. The thrill of the chase, the terror in his victims' eyes, the interrogation room— those were his real rewards. Bhay was a sadist and he didn't care if anyone knew that. That the Supremo had singled him out, he knew. For years, he had excelled wherever fear was necessary. And since Earth's predominant emotion had become fear these days, he had tasted unprecedented success. He just hoped it was a large-scale job.

The door in front of him opened. The Supremo was ready to receive his guest. He strode in, the hunger in his eyes in sharp contrast with his calm demeanor. The room was dark, save for a light at the Supremo's desk. The familiar overpowering stench reached his nostrils. Although he could only see the Supremo, Bhay knew that others were also present.

'You asked for me, Supremo?'

'Ah, Bhay, just the one for the job. Yes, something rather in your line has come up. As you know, our agents on the ground are systematically hunting for the girl Anya Sharma as well as the Enemy. So far, they have both eluded us due to a ridiculous combination of luck and daredevilry, but it won't be long before they are both found. A third front has now opened up, and I want you to take charge of it. General, the impression from the clues, please.'

General Kokh and his aide stepped out of the shadows and motioned the visual to start. The four of them silently watched what the cigarette stub had to say.

'Note the dark red stone on the tiepin' said the Supremo as the last shot zoomed on to the item. 'Your mission is not just to eliminate this man, who is obviously a wordkeeper dedicated to the Enemy's cause, but to also bring me back the red stone. It is vital that I should have it.'

Bhay grunted. A small job. He had hoped for more.

'Why don't you try Mrityu, Supremo? This is more his style.' His voice was like him, a whispered roar, the aggression kept barely under check.

'That may not work out.' Seeing his disappointment, the Supremo added, 'Your quarry is an extremely important part of the resistance, a wordkeeper among wordkeepers. I have good reason to suspect there's more to him than meets the eye. Don't worry, I've sent you an opponent worthy of your powers.'

General Kokh spoke for the first time. 'My office has a file on whatever we know about this man. I'd be happy to share the information with you, Major.' Like everyone except the Supremo, he couldn't bring himself to meet Bhay's gigantic yellow eyes with their tiny irises.

Major Bhay nodded his assent. The three men clicked their heels and bowed to the Supremo, military fashion, before turning and leaving his pod. The rest of the evening would be spent on research with the General and his aide.

In General Kokh's antechamber, coffee was being served after dinner. The staff were always from the prison, and nearly always human, although there were a few yakshas and gandharvas in the mix as well. They were trained and used for service, usually as a reward for good behaviour. The staff had just cleared away the dishes when the General motioned that they be left alone.

After they were alone, he wordlessly gestured at the space in front and a blank rectangle of light appeared. The right half of the rectangle had the same man's face—a grainy image. A dark, dapper gentleman with a military moustache and a shock of white hair stared back at them. He wore a three-piece suit and a tie. The tiepin with its dark red stone was visible to all. As the General spoke, his words appeared as text in the left half of the rectangle.

'Prince Zohrab—industrialist, philanthropist and general bon vivant. Throws a lavish party every year on Diwali, although he's not a religious man and probably not a Hindu. Has a large property near Pachmarhi, practically a whole hill. A bachelor, teetotaller, with an abiding interest in birds. Runs a charitable hospital for them from the Palace grounds.

'Not much is known about him prior to 1970. He is not really an Indian prince. Some offshoot of a minor royal in Fiji, or so his biography says everywhere. He seemed to come from nowhere one fine day in 1970. He made money in every venture of his. To the best of my knowledge, he has no heirs, not even illegitimate ones.'

General Kokh's aide spoke for the first time. 'Take a look at our second file now, Major.' Another rectangle opened up. Prince Zohrab's face filled the right half again, except he was attired in a Sikh turban and bandhgala in a black-and-white daguerrotype. In his turban gleamed a dark, oval stone. A white dove perched on his shoulder.

'Same face, same stone—except it's in Punjab, in 1890. His name—Kartar Singhji, and he was a soldier at Patiala.'

Vikokh was now speeding up his narration. A third window had opened up. The same face stared at them from a portrait. It was of an Awadhi gentleman in court dress. A regal falcon sat on his left wrist.

'1680. A landowner in Awadh. Note the ring.' The dark red stone again.

With a flick of his wrist, General Kokh closed all the windows.

'It is possible, of course, that the men are his ancestors. But each of these men was known to be a bachelor. If they had any family, they were successfully hidden from our agents throughout their lifetime, and their heirs were made wordkeepers in secret. It's a possibility.'

'And the other possibility?' asked Bhay.

'Each man appeared out of nowhere and died

a mysterious death, where their bodies were either not found, or unrecognisable. The other possibility, therefore, is that he's a Chiranjeevi. They would need them on their side, for continuity.'

'In which case, killing him is going to be ...'

'Difficult, not impossible. Once the Enemy is destroyed, the Chiranjeevi are as mortal as the rest of them. He will have more information on their resistance than all the others put together. The Supremo himself tells me that he's their chief strategist. The other wordkeepers will try to contact him sooner or later. We must use this man to find the others. Apart from that, we need his amulet, Major. Some patience and planning will be needed. You will have our considerable capabilities on your side, of course,' added Vikokh.

Bhay snarled and rose to leave. He didn't converse with underlings, twin or no twin. Besides, a plan was forming in his head.

ON THE MOVE

Anya tried on the salwar kameez that Rakshak had brought her. It was large, meant for a fuller person. Well, I'm as thin as a noodle, she thought. He wasn't to know. She hitched up the waistband and gave it an extra roll to tighten it. It would have to stay that way. Needlework wasn't her strong suit.

Rakshak was sitting beside the courtyard of the temple when she emerged. He shook his head in a dissatisfied manner.

'You need to cover your head with a dupatta. You're not going to blend in with your short hair otherwise.'

'I'll never blend in anyway, Rakshak. I look too different, I look like a boy. I should be disguised as a boy, if at all. I'm skinny enough to pass off as one. It's much better.'

Without a word, Rakshak fished out an ancient cutthroat razor from somewhere in his clothing.

'Sit still,' he ordered.

'What are you doing?'

'Shhh,' was the only answer, as he held Anya's head firmly in one hand.

Lock after lock fell off. Finally, satisfied, Rakshak stepped back and said, 'That's better, although I'm no hair stylist.'

Anya desperately searched for a mirror but couldn't find one, so she picked up Rakshak's stainless steel plate and looked into it. She looked different. Very different. Rakshak had given her a crew cut. Her face looked more gaunt this way, harsher. She picked up the small knife he had taught her to use and held it close to her face, so she could see it in the reflection.

The old Anya was dead. Anya the wordkeeper had been born instead.

'It won't do just to barge in and introduce yourself. Zohrab is surrounded by people at all times and any of them might be Kali's minions.' They were walking through the jungle as Rakshak talked. 'Zohrab should approach you—it's not going to be easy for you to meet him—and as I see it, the only way to do that is by letting him see the amulet you're wearing.'

'But if its going to be impossible to meet him, how can he see the amulet in the first place?' asked Anya. She was dressed in her old jeans and t-shirt. A casual observer would see a skinny boy with close cropped hair.

'Which is what today's shopping trip is for.'

'You? You're going shopping with me?'

'No, you're going shopping alone. I tend to stick out, so I'll wait for you at the outskirts of the jungle. You'll need a boy's clothes, shoes—nothing out of the ordinary, remember—and a digital camera with batteries. Use cash only, and move like a boy. Think like one too, especially when you shop. No trying things out for hours.'

'As if! How do you know all this, anyway?'

'Cable,' said Rakshak calmly.

'Well, I know guys who try things out for hours,' argued Anya, annoyed with the remark. Rakshak just smiled his grim smile, refusing to get into an argument.

They had walked to the end of the forest. The bus stop was a hundred yards away, hidden from view by a bend in the road and a cluster of trees at the corner. Anya walked on, hands stuffed in her pockets, head bent down. She was on her own now, for the next couple of hours.

She would need to survive the town.

She concentrated on looking like any other boy on the streets of India. The rest would be a mix of calm, guts and luck.

The Madhya Pradesh Roadways bus to Indore was packed tight. But for a small 'fee', the conductor allowed Anya to ride on top. She clambered up the iron ladder at the back and sat down cross-legged. The bus juddered to life and trundled on.

Anya got the hang of maintaining her balance soon enough. The only tricky part was bending down to avoid the many cables crisscrossing the road. Indore was half an hour away.

She thought of her parents and where they could be at the moment. Were they alive? Somehow Anya was certain of it. But they were, at the very least, in very grave danger, possibly injured, tortured or imprisoned. Anya bit her nails. She needed information on her mother's whereabouts. Ma would know what to do; she always did.

She was certain that the only place where she could find out where her mother was would be Kali's den. The avatar was supposed to lead them there. But how would she find him? She must ask Rakshak. There were some clues to his whereabouts, she knew. What were they? They needed to chase down the clues instead of searching for more wordkeepers,

Prince Zohrab, for instance. Wouldn't it be easier to just search for him online?

Indore bus station came up in the distance. The conductor stopped the bus a good way away from the station and made all the passengers on the top get off before he took the bus in. This was clearly a personal project of his and the driver's.

Anya jumped off the last rung and walked towards the street stalls just outside the station. There were many that sold clothes—shirts, t-shirts, fake leather jackets, cheap sneakers, rubber slippers and the like. She remembered Rakshak's advice and shopped quickly: a few shirts, plain t-shirts, two trousers, a cap, a pair of sneakers, a knapsack, a towel and a pair of sunglasses. Then on second thoughts, she went back and bought extra t-shirts to make bandages out of. Rakshak desperately needed some new ones. Pausing at a second-hand bookstore on the same side of the road, she bought a dog-eared copy of the Mahabharat, suddenly interested in the story of her new friend. No one, except the eccentric and the very poor, read paper books anymore. But she was off the grid. Paper it had to be.

She put on the shirt, sunglasses and cap. She stuffed the rest of her purchases into her knapsack and melted into the crowd.

Relatively confident in her disguise, Anya hailed an auto and headed to the Indrapuri Mall, Indore's latest tourist attraction. She knew there would be close-circuit cameras there, but the digital camera had to be bought—the street stalls didn't have a camera store. At least the mall would be crowded, so she would not be conspicuous.

The security guards let her in without a second look. Anya walked past a large poster with her face on it and 'WANTED' written in large letters underneath. It came as a shock, but she didn't linger or look at it for long. Whoever had put the poster out had used an old photo; she had shoulder-length hair and looked very different. She took the escalator up to the top floor, where the mall guide indicated the electronics goods were sold. A neon sign saying 'Gadget Master' greeted her as she stepped off. Jostled by the crowd, Anya was pushed towards the entrance. An inaugural sale was on and the place was heaving with people. Good.

Buying the camera and batteries was simple. The store attendant was too busy to spend much time with her or any other customer. She left the mall and took an auto to the bus station, realising halfway through her journey that the amulet had somehow come outside her shirt in all the jostling. No harm done, though, she thought, as she quickly tucked it back inside. The auto rattled on through the dusty, crowded road, scurrying past bigger vehicles like an all-surviving cockroach.

Rakshak was waiting for her at the same place he'd dropped her off. He looked at Anya's new outfit and nodded in approval. They set off on their return journey, walking under the cover of the jungle until the fort's ruined outline became visible. He allowed Anya the treat of unpacking her shopping, raising an eyebrow at the gift of t-shirts, but saying nothing. There was work to do. Anya left the book in her knapsack. She felt embarrassed to admit she was curious about him.

'Load the batteries Anya—we need to take some photos.'

For the next fifteen minutes, Ranger clicked away, careful to keep Anya's face in the shadows and focus on the amulet instead. Then he asked Anya to photograph him from a distance. As he stood against the fading light, his gaunt frame and lank hair reminded Anya of a large sal tree. She shivered a little.

That evening, they set out for Pachmarhi. Rakshak did not bother with the usual niceties. Covering Anya's and his own face with a scarf, he held up a roadways bus at gunpoint. Drivers on the jungle route were used to being held up at gunpoint, though. The rule was simple: obey the instructions given. The driver kept his eyes on the road and drove on through the jungle.

Anya found herself nodding off. Her last memory before falling asleep was of Rakshak sitting up straight, his sawn-off rifle pointed at the driver's head.

It was midnight when Rakshak shook her awake. He placed his hand softly over her mouth to warn her not to speak.

Anya looked through the windshield. Silhouettes of sal trees lined the narrow road, looking like warriors gathered up for battle. The high beams of the bus seemed to cleave a path through.

Rakshak was searching for something out there. Whatever it was, he must have found it, for in another minute, he'd nudged the driver with the butt of his rifle and asked him to stop the bus. Keeping the rifle trained on the driver, he let Anya jump off first. Then he leapt off and the two of them ran together into the enveloping darkness of the jungle. The bus driver dialled for help on his mobile, then thought the better of it and disconnected, opting instead to speed on towards a safer stop.

They walked on, with torches to light their way. Rakshak was keen to cross as much of the jungle as possible under the cover of the darkness. The next day, word about their lift would get around soon enough. He wanted Anya to be at Pachmarhi before the office hours started. The bus would take three hours to be out of jungle territory; it would be three am by then. The driver wouldn't dare to call for help within the jungle, he knew. The forest would be swarming with special forces soon after the three hours were over. But they would still have an hour and a half, as it would be dark till four-thirty. Just enough time to make it to the base of the hill.

He walked on like a man possessed by an inner demon. Anya straggled behind, although she was half-running to keep up with his gigantic strides.

'Rakshak, stop!' she finally panted. 'I can't keep up!'

Wordlessly, he picked her up and placed her on his massive shoulders as he strode on, faster than before, now that he didn't have to slow down for her. The lower branches of trees brushed past her cheeks.

Anya dozed off on his shoulders. He let her. She needed her rest for the next bit. Pachmarhi was still an hour and a half away, even at his best speed.

Anya, Anya, Anya my darling ... Find Kalki Anya, find him fast ...

I'm searching, Ma, only I don't know where to look.

You're two sides of the same coin, Anya—just remember that.

Where are you, Ma?

He has me on his Red Planet, Anya—he has me in his prison in his land. Oh I'm so cold here all the time—so alone, so sad, so ... afraid—you can't get here without Kalki.

Don't fret, Ma, don't worry, there's me and Rakshak and Prince Zohrab, soon, and we'll come and rescue you—just hold on for a while.

When, Anya, when? Be careful, I'm so afraid, I hear there's a secret weapon—

'Anya, wake up!' Rakshak shook her arm. Anya hurriedly sat up and immediately wished she hadn't as her head reeled.

'I dreamed of my mother, Rakshak, I talked to her! She's still alive! We've got to save her, Rakshak, we must!'

'Anya, you've got to be brave and face up to the possibility that your mother is dead. It's the realistic thing to do. Had she been alive, she would have definitely tried to contact you.' Rakshak did not look at her as he rearranged the things in his knapsack.

'That's exactly what she did; she contacted me. Through my dream, like you did.'

'That's just wishful thinking on your part, Anya,' said Rakshak, not unkindly. 'We never like to accept that our loved ones have passed on, so our mind makes up scenarios where they are alive.'

'But she was warning me! Rakshak, she was just about to tell me about Kali's secret weapon!'

Rakshak seemed to freeze for a moment, then he continued packing.

'Really, what secret weapon?' he asked in a light voice.

'I don't know, you woke me up just as she was about to tell me!' said Anya, tossing her head.

'Just as well,' said Rakshak. 'You need to concentrate on the task at hand and not bother about dreams. First, we find Prince Zohrab and enlist him. The three of us then go looking for the avatar. Your mother wanted you to do exactly that, not run off on a wild goose chase for a weapon.

'Now listen carefully, without interrupting. I will take you to the outskirts of the Prince's property. You have to drop this envelope with the memory card in his office, then wait for him to approach you.

'I'll be right here every evening. Just come by after dusk. And remember, there probably will be spies all around the Prince.'

Anya took the envelope addressed to the Prince, turned away from Rakshak and walked up the hill road. Dawn was breaking over the horizon. She now knew why Rakshak had insisted on her travelling alone to Indore. That was the dress rehearsal.

AN ALLY AT LAST

The Prince's estate included an entire hill and the valleys on all sides. Anya found herself gaping at the vast expanse of land owned by the man. In this day and age, who knew of such landowners?

Small homes dotted the hillside. Many of them were adorned by a photograph of the natty old gentleman in his three-piece suit, often with a marigold garland hanging from it. She walked up the dirt path that led through the village and seemed to go all the way up to the palace.

The whole hill was alive with birds of all kinds. Every home had a perch and two bowls for birds to rest, quench their thirst and feed. There were nests on every tree. I wonder if the prince is a bird lover, she thought.

Her question was answered at the next turn in the road. A giant billboard welcomed her to 'Pakshi Vihar—the garden of birds'. The prince's smiling face was alongside the text.

Reading on, Anya realised that Pakshi Vihar was a free hospital for birds. The notice proclaimed that Pakshi Vihar was headed and managed by the prince himself.

A germ of an idea began to form in Anya's mind.

She walked on through the village, looking for signs to Pakshi Vihar. This was more difficult than it appeared. But finally, Anya stopped a passer-by on his way to the temple and asked. He directed her to the next village. The hospital opened at six in the morning and shut at four in the afternoon. Yes, the prince visited every day. No, he didn't know much else about the prince. Just that he was immensely popular, and a bird lover, and that people on the hill welcomed birds as a mark of their respect for him. The prince had personally overseen the development of each village on the hill. The people had not forgotten.

Mulling over her newly-acquired information, Anya wondered how the wordkeeper took the risk of having such a public profile. The prince's photographs were plastered everywhere, yet, there he was, alive and unharmed and apparently unconcerned enough to wear his amulet in full view and to turn up at his bird hospital on a daily basis.

She was halfway up the hill when she reached the gates of Pakshi Vihar. It couldn't have been later than seven-thirty in the morning, yet there were already a fair number of people there, along with birds of every possible size and description. Anya sat on a wooden bench, next to a woman with a rooster on her lap. The rooster looked balefully at Anya, then walked up towards her and scrutinised her, first with his left eye, then with his right. Apparently satisfied, he uttered a soft cluck and gently pecked his owner's chin. She smiled at him with great affection and looked at Anya.

'He just won't go into the hen coop,' she said, without a preamble. 'Panics the moment I put him in there, instead of, you know, doing whatever he's supposed to do. I've got him here to find out if anything can be done.'

Anya smiled mechanically at the woman as her thoughts raced in dangerous directions. Maybe he's a confirmed bachelor, she thought, maybe he's gay. Maybe your hens are seriously ugly—yep, the real plain janes of the hen world. She smiled at the thought, forgetting where she was for a moment. The woman was saying something.

'Er, what?'

'Your bird, boy. Where's your bird?'

'What bird? Oh—no, no, I didn't bring a bird for the prince, just some photos. Of birds,' she hastily added, in case she sounded unconvincing.

'Oh that? You don't need to wait here for that, lad, just go into his office—through those doors there—and leave them there with a note.'

Anya mumbled something about security. The woman smiled a broad smile.

'This is the prince's land, son. Not like the rest of the country. Just leave them there. The prince'll see them when he gets to the hospital.'

Anya walked through the double doors at the end of the corridor and sat at the marble-topped desk in the corner of a cool room, painted in sea green distemper and cream oil paint. It was strangely soothing. Taking a pen from the pen stand, she scribbled her message on the notepad. Then she stepped out of the empty office and strode casually towards the door. So far, so good.

Now for some breakfast. And the Mahabharat, if time permitted.

The prince sat frozen at his desk, staring unblinkingly at the screen. It was impossible to see the face from the photographs; the boy was against the light, his face turned away from the lens. But the amulet was visible clearly enough, swinging clean from the boy's torso as he bent forward a little. The Rakshak had contacted him decades ago, asking him to prepare for this day. Did this really mean the avatar had come? Or was it a trap set out by those who didn't know that Balram was a girl?

He looked at the hastily scribbled note. 'Back in three hours. Find me in the garden.' Garden probably meant the recovery area of the hospital—a two-acre space, where the birds spent time healing once they were freed from the hospital cages. They flew away when they felt well enough.

The prince smiled to himself. No one in his family had liked birds; his elder brother had famously killed one, in fact, but he had loved them wholeheartedly. They had remained his friends over the years.

He looked at his wristwatch. The boy should be here by now. Putting the flash drive and the piece of paper in his pocket, he stepped out for a walk.

He was standing between two amaltas trees, intently watching a small red bird. The prince walked as silently as a cat until he was touching distance away, then said, 'It's a red-whiskered bulbul from the Himalayas. You find them this far down south only when winter sets in. This one is recovering from a broken wing, that's why he's still around.'

It was when his guest jumped with a hand on his heart that he realised he was in the presence of a girl. A certain delicacy of features was suggested from the silhouette in the photos, though it was not conclusive.

But her unguarded start with that soft swish of the hand gave her away her femininity.

He caught his breath sharply. The young wordkeeper, safe, at his doorstep, as originally planned! Relief flooded over him like soothing waves of water. Keeping his voice steady, he spoke.

'My dear child, if you're going to be in disguise, you've got to become the person you're disguised as. At all moments, especially the unguarded ones.'

Unfazed, she said, 'Amulet'. She'd already fished hers out from inside the shirt. The prince took off his tie pin and held it in his hand. The two stones gleamed blood red for an instant, seeming to recognise each other. She nodded at him and put hers back inside her shirt.

'I'm Anya.'

'Zohrab. Pleased to meet you at last, Anya.'

'You've heard of me?'

'The young wordkeeper who will guide everyone to the avatar? You're part of the legend, Anya.'

'That's ridiculous. I have no clue where he is. You might as well know that right away.'

'Well, prophecies have a strange way of panning out. Shall we just agree to wait and see?' he said with a smile.

'Zohrab—is it a Parsi name?'

'It's a prince's name,' he said, his face impassive.

'Sounds like a made-up name to me.'

Ignoring the last remark, the prince said, 'You will join my staff as a trainee. I will train you in the ways of the hospital, as I train all my other staff. That'll be the best camouflage, I feel. Have you thought of a name and a background story? You'll need one.'

'I wasn't planning to stay that long. I'm here just to pick you up, so we can go and meet Rakshak. The longer I stay, the riskier it is for you. We need the cover of the jungle for safety. We had to hijack a bus to get here, and I'll bet you anything they've put two and two together by now and are coming for us.'

'Still, for the next few hours, you're Manoj. Decide what your story is. When are we meeting Rakshak?'

'This evening, at dusk. I know the place. I don't like the name Manoj.'

The prince ignored this remark as well.

For the next six hours, Anya learnt the basics about nursing birds—how to tie a tiny splint for a wing bone fracture on a sparrow, the correct medicine dosage for birds of different sizes, the way food is mashed up and chewed before giving the slushy mix to baby birds. The prince was clearly at his happiest when looking after them, in spite of all his other identities.

Finally, just before four in the evening, he took Anya to his personal aviary. Anya's eyes were so dazzled by the collective brilliance of the plumage that she had to blink a couple of times.

'These are my birds,' he said proudly, almost like a little boy showing off his car collection. 'Each one of them has elected to stay with me. I haven't put them in cages or coops. Some just visit me now and then and some are permanent residents. And this one is my personal favourite.'

A regal falcon had just unlatched the door to his large coop with his beak. He waddled up, as birds do, before hopping on to Anya's shoulder and glaring at her—balefully again—with one eye. Then he repeated the action with Anya's other shoulder and his other eye. Finally, satisfied, he flew the short distance to Prince Zohrab's shoulder, where he paid no further attention to Anya and focussed on cleaning his talons instead.

'Garud is trained to follow, search and find me. You must have heard of the falcon's exceptional eyesight and its ability to fly long distances. Therefore, he is also my most trusted and successful messenger.' He affectionately stroked the bird's head as he spoke, making the falcon close its eyes in delight.

'Here's what I want us to do, Anya. We will give our amulets to him for safekeeping, just in case the enemy catches up with us. He can find us and deliver the amulets once we're in a safe place, and he *will* do that. That's what he's trained to do.

'What will he do with them?' asked Anya.

'Well, he'll swallow them, and then, in due course of time, you know, they'll come out,' said the prince, looking at the ceiling as he spoke.

Anya glanced doubtfully at the bird, who seemed unconcerned, looking for all the world that he had been excreting vital clues all his life.

'Fine. Let's do it then.'

They took off their amulets and gave them to the bird, who swallowed them whole. The prince told one of the hospital assistants that he was heading out for a spot of twitching with Manoj. Since the prince didn't seem the nervous kind, and the assistant took it very matter-of-factly, Anya guessed this meant bird-watching.

They got into a small Mercedes and drove down the hill. Garud followed the car from high above.

Driving down the hill took an hour, as the road wound round. It was nearly dusk when Anya and the prince were at the outskirts of the jungle.

'Leave the car here, it won't go in any deeper,' said Anya.

They walked through the sal trees lining the edge of the forest. The trees grew thicker with every step, making the dusk look darker than it already was. Anya felt a whisper of a breath on her shoulder and heard a soft voice murmur.

'Careful.'

'Did you say something?' she asked the prince in an undertone, turning round. To her surprise, he was a good three yards behind her. I'm beginning to hear stuff in my head again, she thought. This can't be good.

She cautiously walked on a little further, looking for her friend.

He was standing very still beside one of the many sal trees—so still that he seemed a part of it. Even Anya, who had been seeing him every day, nearly walked past him, sensing rather than seeing him at first. The prince realised his presence when he heard the deliberate rustle next to his ear.

He had barely altered, although someone had recently changed his bandages. The wordkeeper, presumably. So finally the loner had a friend, he thought. Good for him. He's suffered enough.

'We meet again, Rakshak.'

'Hush, let's move further in. This is far too public.'

The three of them ploughed deeper into the jungle, Garud following them high in the sky.

Night had well and truly fallen when Rakshak stopped in front of a ravine. A deep river had once flowed through it. It was now bone dry, but the bed was still deep. He motioned them down some roughly hewn steps on the side. There, burrowed underneath the bank, was a clearing. Rakshak had evidently been hiding out here, for he had collected firewood and heaped it into a pile.

They sank down gratefully on the ground, stretching their limbs. After drinking deeply from Rakshak's leather flask, Anya dug into the food available—fruits, and some wood-roasted root vegetables that Rakshak had made earlier.

'Wild garlic, onions and sweet potatoes,' he explained. 'I had planted some years ago. They're still feeding me.' Then, very cautiously, he lit the fire. 'I can't build it up much. The existing canopy and this depth will camouflage a small fire, but not a crackling one.'

'I think it's wonderful,' said Anya, quite honestly. She had already begun to yawn.

The prince lit up a slim cheroot and inhaled.

'So let's come to the point. Where are we now?'

'Finding the avatar,' replied Anya.

'Does anyone have any clues?'

Anya hesitated, then shook her head. All she had was a bunch of dreams, a warning and whispers in the wind. She didn't want the prince to think she was insane or the neurotic type in less than twelve hours after meeting her.

'I don't have any clues about the avatar's whereabouts, but I have an idea of where Kali's lair might be,' said Rakshak in his measured manner.

The moment seemed to freeze. Anya sat up straight. The prince stopped inhaling and stared at Rakshak. Even Garud cocked his head to one side, immobile. The only thing moving was the flames.

AMBUSH AND RESCUE

'You must know of the Earth's unique position in the cosmos?' said Rakshak.

'Do you mean the Gatekeeper legend?'

'What's the Gatekeeper legend?' asked Anya.

Prince Zohrab spoke after glancing at Rakshak, as if to take his permission.

'There's an old tale among the Jangil tribes of Andaman. They claimed they were gatekeepers or guards of heaven's door. They believed that there is a gateway into other worlds from one of their islands—a gateway that would take you to heaven.'

'But surely it's just another folktale, like all the other myths of the world?'

'The Jangil tribe died out in 1905, so they can't defend themselves, Anya,' Rakshak spoke, absently stoking the fire with a stick. 'The Jangil happened to believe it was true. So do I, for that matter.'

'Why?'

'Because I've seen it with my own eyes.'

The prince's eyes narrowed in disbelief just as Anya's went as round as saucers. Rakshak smiled at the contrasting faces and continued, 'It was a long, long time ago—nearly five thousand years ago. After the war, I ran away from my homeland in the north with my cursed face and body. Wherever I sought shelter, I was repulsed. It seemed that all of India, right up to the Narmada valley, was aware of what I had done and was determined to punish me. I travelled far and wide and eventually walked southward, resigned to my fate as an outcast. Here, people were still repulsed by my wound, but at least they felt pity. I was grateful even for that. They left food for me outside, wherever I stayed—abandoned huts, crematoriums, ruined temples—for no one would shelter me. I stayed nowhere for long, spending between one to three months in every village as I made my way towards the coast. Eventually, the story of the curse filtered down there as well, and I became less and less welcome. Villagers started hounding me out after a few years because they felt I was unlucky for them.

'Luckily, I had prepared for such a day and had crafted myself a small boat, which I had kept hidden off the Coromandel coast. One moonless night, I silently set sail in the little boat, towards some islands that I knew existed in the southeast. It was said that they were haunted and the tribals who stayed there ate humans, so I knew no one would willingly follow me there. And if there were people staying there at all, I was hoping they wouldn't have heard of me. Any chance of a place to live was good enough.'

'Did you have any regrets about what you'd done—you know, in the war?'

'No, not then, anyway. I was still trying just to survive. It hadn't yet sunk in that I would survive come what may. I thought a lot about those last days of the war, once everyone from my old life had gone and a new, terrifyingly lonely world had taken its place. No, I stand by what I did, Anya. Everyone had crossed boundaries in the war. But there were days when ...' His voice trailed off.

'Anyway, I sailed for several days and nights and eventually my little boat docked at a green island. It looked peaceful and welcoming—a paradise of sorts. I dragged my tired self to the shore and immediately fell asleep. Next morning, I saw that I was on one of the smaller islands of an archipelago. I walked around the place in three hours or so. It was uninhabited. The island had fruit orchards and enough coconut palms to sustain me. In a week, I made myself a small thatched shelter. It was the closest I had been to happiness in years. Peace at last.

'And then, a month into my stay, I was ambushed in my sleep. A horde of twenty or so tribal soldiers attacked me, bound me hand and foot and took me to their leader. I couldn't understand a word of what was being said. It was very apparent that he was furious. He kept pointing at the sky so I assumed I had offended their gods in some way. Well, the upshot of that was that I was sentenced to death. They gave me a bath and put me in clean clothes, after which I was made to climb a platform of sorts where I was to be executed. The whole village was uttering strange chants mixed with clicking sounds, while we waited for the executioner. To calm my terrified mind, I took a few gulping breaths and looked up at the sky, trying to avoid the gloating faces underneath. And then I saw it.'

A clattering sound startled them all. Prince Zohrab had dropped the stone he was playing with on the hard ground.

'Saw what?' asked Anya in a hoarse whisper.

'The gateway to the Red Planet.'

'The Red Planet?' Anya blurted out. But that's ...'

'Careful, careful, careful,' the fire seemed to crackle. The flames reminded her of a bird's wings. She stopped.

Rakshak looked at her, alert, eyes narrowed. 'Go on.'

'I was going to say that it could be Mars,' lied Anya.

'Could be,' said Rakshak, losing interest.

'The myth was real. It just seemed a dull red streak in the sky at first. When I looked closely, I saw something move—a red stone rolled across. I realised it was a distinct separate entity, not of or from Earth at all. There it was, right above my head, a portion of sky that seemed really close. I could reach it if I stretched. I took my chances and jumped up at the red streak. The gateway sucked me in—its gravitational pull wrenching me away from certain death. I travelled very briefly through a layer of gases, then I was hurled to the ground in this new world. From where I was, I could see the astonished faces of the islanders gaping up at me. The Earth seemed blue-green, and was becoming distant every minute. The new planet was spinning away from it at a tremendous speed. I was in a new world.

'I called it the Red Planet in my head; everything was red or a dusty red. Five red moons, red earth, red stones, muddy red water. A dusty red breeze was blowing. I marked my landing spot with a fallen branch from an unfamiliar tree and started exploring the planet.

'The whole place smelt as if something had been

rotting for a while. I walked on for a good few hours and saw nobody. The place had no buildings of any kind, no dwellings. Just large holes leading to tunnels burrowed under the ground. I felt someone's presence, but never saw him.'

'What kind of presence?'

'A malevolent presence, concentrated hatred. It's hard to explain. I felt uneasy, restless, on edge and then, unreasonably angry. I wanted to hit out, kill, exact revenge on people. Had there been anyone present, I might have committed yet another murder. Except there was no one. Just a hint of someone watching me.

'I stepped into a tunnel, which went deep into the ground. The stench was stronger there, almost unbearable. Also the feeling of hatred, anger, evil— that was overwhelming.

'I came back to the surface, and stayed there for the rest of my stint on the planet. I'd realised a strange thing: even if my life was endangered and cursed, I still wanted to live on familiar Earth, not on this alien land.'

'How did you get back?'

'I found my way back to the spot I had marked and bided my time there. The Red Planet came close to Earth once every fortnight. The first fortnight, I just observed the green and blue streak, not prepared to jump back. It went away in a flash. I guarded the spot rigorously every day after that, sustaining myself on some strange fruit and the reddish water. The streak reappeared exactly fourteen days later, and I jumped. The same sucking sensation engulfed me, then I was thrown back on to familiar Earth soil. When I looked up, I saw the red streak diminishing second by second before my eyes.'

'What happened with the islanders?'

'They left me alone after that. They probably thought it was inauspicious to harm someone who had returned from the gateway. Anyway, I was allowed to stay on the island. They visited once a month for their special rituals and left me fruits and food as a token of their friendship. Over the years, I got to know their language a little. They were a tribe called the Jangil. They called me Aka-Bea, the foreigner. That's how I heard their legend.'

'What does it say?'

'They say that over the years, when the injustices of this world have crossed tipping point, the heavens will part, and a great saviour will come through the gateway. He will be seated on a flying horse and will rid us of evil with his flaming sword. He will save the good, including the Jangil, who have guarded his gates from the beginning of time. Sounds familiar?'

'Why didn't they think you were their saviour?' asked the prince.

'No flying horse, no flaming sword—just an unceremonious crash landing,' smiled Rakshak. 'Not divine enough, Prince.'

'Was there anything there at all on the Red Planet, that seemed remotely like a powerful entity like the saviour?' asked Anya.

'Whatever was there, was no saviour. It was evil, pure and simple,' answered Rakshak firmly.

Anya yawned, stretching out like a cat. 'Some bedtime story,' she said. 'I think I'll turn in for the night, if you don't mind.' She waved good night, curled up in a ball close to the fire and was immediately fast asleep.

The two men sat in companionable silence, smoking the prince's cheroots.

'It must have been about five thousand years ago. Will you recognise it if you see it again?' Prince Zohrab's voice was barely audible. They were taking care not to wake Anya.

'I stayed on the island for a hundred years. I know the night sky by heart. Of course I will.'

'Will the locals let you?'

'The last of the Jangils died out in 1905. No one knows of the gateway any more, or where it used to be. Except me. You see, I taught myself cartography in the last two centuries. All that time on my hands. And while I was waiting for all the signs of the saviour to emerge, as background work, I revisited my island to find out its coordinates. 92°E and 11°N.'

'92°E and 11°N? But that's—'

'Port Blair. I know. So the sleepy island of five thousand years ago is now a crowded capital city. But that alters nothing. Have you ever seen the night sky at Port Blair? There's a red streak running across it. Locals think it's light pollution, but the old tribals know better.'

'On the Red Planet ... it was him, wasn't it? You felt Kali that day.'

'I didn't want to discuss it in front of Anya. But I really know what the presence of Kali feels like. People think that I deliberately killed an unborn child out of spite. Naturally. They saw me do it. But what they don't know was that that was not my natural self at all. In those last days of the war, I was not myself. Something had started living in me, possessing all my faculties and divorcing judgement and my conscience from all my decisions. After being on the Red Planet, I knew what the overpowering sensation of those days had been. I had been possessed by Kali that day on the battlefield.

'I think Krishna knew, which is why he cursed

me, hoping to trap the beast for all eternity within me. Somehow, Kali escaped and I regained my sense of self. I am not saying this to absolve myself of all responsibility of the crime. I serve my sentence without complaint. But I was definitely controlled by some other malevolent force that held sway over me for a period. I felt it.

'Krishna eventually recaptured him, you know. Shut him up in tiny formlessness on a different galaxy.'

'And you're suggesting that that place is the Red Planet?'

'Either that, or the planet he managed to escape to. Kali didn't dare to return to Earth for as long as Krishna lived. But that was a bare fifty more years. Kali Yug started when Krishna passed away. I think he has been building his own army while he was waiting out there.

'And one more thing. He's got at least one wordkeeper captive, alive—out there. Her mother.' He nodded towards Anya.

'What? How do you know, Rakshak?'

'Shh, softly ... you know amulets change colour when they are passed from one wordkeeper to another?'

'Actually, I've never had the experience, since I've

never had to pass it on to another.' Prince Zohrab sounded apologetic.

'I forget, you're like me. For normal mortals, an amulet changes colour when a wordkeeper dies and the new wordkeeper takes charge of it. The colour changes from red to crystal clear and slowly goes back to red as the new owner wears it for a while. It's the amulet's way of getting accustomed to a new owner. Well, for Anya, the colour never changed at all. Which means her mother is still out there somewhere, alive. My belief is that she is with Kali as his prisoner.'

Prince Zohrab stroked his chin. 'That's exactly what he wants! Don't you see, her mother would be the ideal bait for luring Anya in, amulet and all! That's why we need to find the avatar first. We need some more numbers; we need his strength before we can confront Kali. He's not going to kill Tanya Sharma as long as he is searching for Anya and her amulet.'

CRASH!

The forest around her seemed to burst with noise all at once. Many explosions; bullets whizzing past her head.

Anya felt herself swept up by a pair of powerful hands as the prince lifted her up and ran into the jungle. He fumbled inside his jacket and took out a small automatic. She turned around desperately and got a split second view of a large, gaunt frame, tied to seven huge trees—new wounds gaping open within the old—eyes swollen shut.

As if sensing her presence, Rakshak shook himself from his stupor and yelled, 'Anya, run! It's a trap!'

Jumping from the prince's arms, she blindly ran ahead, deeper into the jungle, aware of a rumbling sound above her. Looking up, she saw three smoking clouds rushing towards her through the sky, rapidly forming into shapes, then faces, the largest one in the middle. It had a gigantic cruel face and enormous, lidless yellow eyes. And those eyes had just seen her.

She grabbed the prince by the hand and yanked him into thicker forest, seeking the cover of trees. But the clouds were faster. They swerved slightly to correct their course, their torsos forming as they flew closer, their unimaginably large mouths emitting flames that engulfed the trees behind the fugitives.

Anya felt something snap inside her. All her fear seemed to be replaced with a blind fury. I will not die a coward's death, she thought grimly. If this is what its going to come to, Anya Sharma will fight her way out or fight to the end. I don't know if there's an avatar at all or not, I don't know if I can still save my mother, but it really doesn't matter right now. This is about who I am. And Anya Sharma doesn't leave her friends behind and run.

She swivelled round, fishing for her trusty knife inside her waistband and started running back towards Rakshak in a zigzag fashion to avoid the shower of fire around her, as he had taught her. Beside her, Prince Zohrab was guarding her back, shooting at the clouds with his left hand and swiping to clear the branches with the sword in his right hand.

Anya cleaved a path through a thicket. She was now behind Rakshak. She and the prince started cutting through the tough ropes that bound him. It was a horribly slow process. The terrible trio in the sky were almost complete now, their legs forming.

'Don't cut, burn!' shouted the prince, handing her a flaming branch. Anya set the ropes on fire with a short prayer in her head.

It worked. Rakshak's bonds fell away and he leaped up like a coiled snake. Hoisting Anya and the prince on each shoulder as if they were weightless, he ran helter-skelter through the forces into deeper forest.

No one knew these forests better than Rakshak. He had spent several centuries here, had planted some of its oldest trees with his own hands, had created decoys where none had existed. He had shaped the forest as it stood today.

Very soon, the three of them were in a clearing with a thick leafy canopy above it.

Inside the clearing stood the strangest woman Anya had ever seen—part mad old woman muttering to herself, part calendar goddess. There was a crow on her shoulder. She was pacing up and down the length of the clearing while pulling incessantly on a cigarette.

Seeing Prince Zohrab, she threw the cigarette down. 'I came as soon as I could. Is Balram here? How long do we have?'

Rakshak responded, 'Five minutes on the outside before they find us. It's not far, just hidden.'

'And that's Balram, is it? Well, come on then,' she said, yanking Anya towards her with a reedy arm.

'Wait!' said the prince, stopping her. 'How do we know you can be trusted?'

'But I'm a girl!' said Anya at the same time.

The woman went slightly madder at this commotion and wailed, 'Why, in the name of our creative father, is Balram inevitably slow? In every yug!' She calmed herself with an effort and turned to the prince. 'You need my help to face them;

they're far too powerful for the three of you. Trust me. Plus, right now you're dead either way, so you can't lose.'

There was no time to argue, so Anya kept quiet, now certain that the crazy woman would be responsible for killing them all. Dhoomavati just held Anya's head in her hands and asked her to close her eyes. Fearing another crazy outburst, and keen to hurry up the process, Anya did as she was told.

A whirlwind of images appeared in the spot between her eyebrows. A village in the hills, a Buddhist village with lamas, then a long journey through Nepal, Uttarakhand and Uttar Pradesh, ending in a southern Indian town—no, not a town, a village. Then, then she strained to see the next bit—a journey to the east, crossing state borders, hills, forests, familiar forests from her dreams ...

'Mahendra Giri. That's where he is,' said Dhoomavati and clapped her hands. Things happened at breathtaking speed: the crow on Dhoomavati's shoulder hopped off and grew until it was as big as a small lorry; all four of them climbed on, and just as they were flying off, a searing pain tore through Anya's arm, as a bullet finally found its target.

Kali's forces were rushing in, Dambha noticeably with a scar right down the middle, but it was too late for them. Far more menacing were the three enormous demons with one arm who were swooping in on them, flying much faster than their crow.

Dhoomavati, unperturbed, lit another cigarette, took a drag and exhaled. Hard. Thick clouds of smoke engulfed their bird. Taking advantage of the camouflage, the crow flew higher until it disappeared into the clouds.

Anya's ears were ringing. The last thing that she remembered was Prince Zohrab grabbing her arm as she slumped forward in a dead faint.

ANYA AND BILAL

... planning to use against the messiah ... I am so scared of my thoughts here, Anya—they are awful, I can only seem to think of bad things happening, some days I feel I'm losing my mind.

No, Ma, no! Just hang in there, Ma and I'll come and get you, I promise. There's more of us now, the prince and Rakshak and a lady who flies, and we're so close to finding him, you've got to hang on.

Come quickly, Anya, before my mind becomes his. I'm so afraid he'll take it and control it.

Think happy thoughts, Ma, like our picnics in the garden and I'll be there before—

Someone was slapping her awake. Anya's face felt wet.

'There! That's better!' said Dhoomavati. 'We were afraid we'd lost you.' Her repulsive gap-toothed smile made Anya shudder. She knew this monstrous woman (was she human at all?) had saved her life, but she found her terrifying, nonetheless.

Blood poured out from Anya's wound in a steady stream, making her head spin when she looked at it.

'It's just a flesh wound, but the bullet's no ordinary bullet. It wasn't made by humans, for a start. I've put a bandage on it for the time being, but I need to find the actual medicine to heal that wound.' She spoke the words lightly enough, but Anya could sense from the frown on her forehead that Dhoomavati was worried.

Anya was shivering with cold, her teeth chattering. She looked around feebly, trying to locate the others. She was inside a cave. Through its entrance, Anya could see that the giant crow had assumed normal proportions and was perched on a branch with his head tucked under his wing. Rakshak was sitting a little way away, his large torso leaning against a tree. The prince was nowhere to be seen.

Dhoomavati took out a winnow from her ragged bundle, and some rice.

'Curse this rice! It's been doing that every single time today. Strange. We must have left them far behind by now.'

Anya looked inquiringly at her. She felt too weak to speak.

'It's the winnow,' explained Dhoomavati. 'The rice grains keep forming the letter "sha" for "shatru" and a knife, warning signs for enemies at close range. But I know this cave is hidden from all eyes and safe—so how can that be? Anyway, your medicine's more important.' She peered at the grains for a while longer, then looked at Anya with a strange expression in her eyes. It was not her usual red-hot fury at all. What was it—pity? Anya stared back.

'The thing is, girl, that the wound here is caused by something not belonging to Earth, and nothing on Earth can cure it. I suspect it's from his land, Vishasha—and the medicine will be found there as well. If something isn't done soon, the wound will gradually poison your blood. Now, no one knows where Vishasha is, not even me, although I've been taken there several times. So I'm guessing we won't be able to get there, at least not in time to save you. There is only one other way to cure you if I discount Vishasha.'

'What?' whispered Anya.

'Holding all ten amulets close to your body. The amulets have miraculous healing properties, but one is too feeble for your wound. The more amulets you wear, the faster you heal.'

As if on cue, the prince and Rakshak entered the cave, the prince holding two freshly washed amulets in his hand. Garud waddled in behind them, looking rather pleased with himself.

'Didn't I tell you he was marvellous? Look, both amulets, and not a feather out of place,' the prince beamed like a proud parent.

'Quick, bring them here,' said Dhoomavati. She almost snatched them from his hands and put them on Anya.

'Of course!' murmured Rakshak in a soft voice.

Anya felt instantly better. Her head was still swimming, but she was able to sit up and examine her arm. The blood from her arm had stopped gushing, and was now just a trickle. A comfortable warmth stole round her heart and spread to other parts of her body, although her extremities were still freezing.

'I want to save my mother! I know you know, Rakshak, and I'm going to get out and fetch her and ...' She was too tired to fight any more.

'That'll have to do for now, she's fit enough to fly. Karkash!'

The crow pulled his head out from under his wing and hopped down from the tree. He swelled to his earlier size. The four of them sat astride him, the whoosh of his flapping wings unimaginably loud in their ears. Garud soared high up in the sky, following his master.

In spite of the stunning, silent beauty of the night, Dhoomavati found herself searching the horizon in all directions for the enemy that the winnow had predicted.

They flew for a few hours. Mahendra Giri gleamed blue-green in the misty light of dawn. As Karkash swooped down, preparing to land, Anya, now conscious, saw small huts in the thickest part of the jungle, cleverly camouflaged to avoid detection. The tiny settlement seemed to blend in with the browns and greens of its immediate surroundings.

A group of teenagers—boys and girls—ran out to meet them, guns cocked at the sky. The noise made by Karkash's wings must have alerted them, thought Anya.

One of them shouted, 'Stop! You may not land without our permission. Identify yourselves!'

Dhoomavati, furious, screwed her red eyes up and was going to blast them away in a cloud of foul-smelling smoke, but the prince intervened.

'Anya, you must show yourself with the two amulets, otherwise they'll shoot us right away!'

'I need to speak to the leader of your village,' yelled Anya, as loudly and commandingly as she could manage. 'I am a wordkeeper, and I can prove it. I am also seriously injured and need shelter.'

'Just you, then,' said the boy who had called out

earlier. He seemed to be leading the pack. 'The rest must stay up there until we verify that the wordkeeper is genuine.'

Karkash hovered even lower, almost touching the ground, so Anya could jump off. She managed to do so with the last vestiges of strength left in her, although the nerves inside her head jangled harshly with the impact of her feet on the ground.

A middle-aged man had stepped out from one of the huts on hearing the commotion. He was dressed in fatigues like a soldier, but also, incongruously, wore three ash stripes on his forehead. A machine gun hung casually from his belt.

'Sir, this girl says she is a wordkeeper,' said the leader, keeping the gun trained on Anya's forehead as he spoke.

The man parted the small crowd and stepped forward. He rolled up a sleeve to reveal his blood-red amulet.

'Now yours,' he said to Anya.

She took out her chain and pendant, to which she had attached the tiepin so both stones could touch her skin. All three amulets gleamed bright red in mutual recognition.

'Sorry. It's a precaution against shapeshifters. Welcome,' said the man.

Anya just nodded and sat down under the nearest tree. She felt drained again.

The entourage, circling the skies above like a weird helicopter, was finally allowed to land. Before anyone could say a word, Dhoomavati rushed to Anya, cradling her head on her lap. The change from fearsome, eccentric goddess to mother figure was striking.

'She's not just any wordkeeper, Bhargav, she is Balram. And she is grievously injured.'

'Balram—a girl?' said the man, smiling a slight smile, perhaps at some past memory. 'How could you tell?'

'Balram is the key. Only Balram is supposed to know where the avatar will be. In spite of that, I tried, being a goddess and all that, but it was of no use. The avatar's exact location remained stubbornly hidden. Must be one of the safeguards against Kali, after all, he is a god too. All that the winnow was willing to show me was a path to Balram. And him, of course,' she said, pointing at Ashwatthama as he bowed from a distance. Dhoomavati continued, 'So I flew in, right in the middle of an ambush by Kali's agents.'

'And she knew everything?'

'Not consciously, no. It was all locked in her subconscious. I had to tap into her dreams to get the information. Enough now! I need your amulet immediately, for her. She's been hit by a Vishasha bullet.'

Parashuram understood the gravity of the order. He took his amulet off at once, severing it from the string with a knife. As Dhoomavati attached it with the other two, a surge of energy swept through Anya. She finally had the strength to speak and sit up.

'The avatar, where is he?'

'Well, that's what we have Ashwatthama here for, isn't it? After all, that's the one thing none of us can do—recognise him through a miracle.' Bhargav spoke with a tinge of sarcasm in his voice. Anya felt rather annoyed at this slight at her friend. Rakshak had more than proved himself. But this was not the time for arguing.

Without a word, Rakshak stepped forward and walked towards the line of boys, now standing at ease in rows, army fashion. If the boys flinched at the sight of his oozing, sore-filled body, they didn't show it.

As Rakshak walked past the first four boys and faced the fifth, his face underwent a dramatic change. The oozing sores shrank and disappeared; the hole on his forehead very gradually started to close up.

The boy in front of him frowned as Rakshak knelt in front of him, staring with furious concentration at his hands as his alabaster skin regained its lustre. Rakshak stood up, smiling slightly as he placed his hand on the boy's shoulder. The avatar had finally been found. Then he walked away into the distance, far from the group.

Anya gasped in surprise, she could barely recognise the handsome warrior. It's all been too emotional for him, she thought.

'Come out then, Bilal,' said his teacher.

Anya looked at the fair boy with his high cheekbones and serious expression; she was quivering from head to foot in excitement. It was evident to her and everyone present that they looked remarkably alike. The only difference was in their complexions; he was as fair as ivory, whereas she was the colour of filter coffee with milk.

'Twins! The children are twins!' exclaimed Prince Zohrab.

'Are you Anya?' asked Bilal, stepping up and staring at her face. He pronounced it as 'uh-nya', meaning 'the other one' in Sanskrit. Anya immediately knew that that must have been her original name. Anya was an effort to hide her identity and help her blend in with everyone else. She nodded, shyly.

'You must be ... Kalki,' she said, suddenly getting the last missing piece from her dreams. 'Your name is Kalki, not Bilal.'

They hugged each other, tentatively at first, then tightly as they realised they had found family at last. Then, blinking away his tears, Bilal took out his own amulet and put it round his sister's neck.

THE SECRET WEAPON

That evening was festive; everyone in Parashuram's camp gathered around the fire, forming little clusters of conversation. Dhoomavati had created a smoke screen above the canopy of trees, so the little village could not be seen from above. The army that Parashuram commanded had prepared arrack and there were quite a few slightly drunk, happy faces around.

Sitting in one of the clusters were Dhoomavati, Prince Zohrab, Parashuram, Bilal, Ashwatthama and Anya. The prince had taken his shoes off and was warming his feet at the fire. His feet reminded Anya of something, but she couldn't quite remember what.

The adults were a few drinks down, barring the prince, who was just delirious with happiness. Dhoomavati had conspicuously drunk half the arrack herself, but Bilal and Anya had sipped it and put their glasses away. It tasted and smelt vile. They were too scared to refuse Dhoomavati, however, and kept pouring the stuff surreptitiously under a nearby bush.

Anya moved closer to Dhoomavati, who regarded her with a cloudy stare. 'Sit down child, what have you got to ask? They're all asking away about the future.'

'There's something I don't understand.' She hesitated, because the Seer was looking extra eccentric at that moment. 'My mother ... she mentioned having seen him, you know, the avatar, as a child. In her letter to me, I mean,' she added.

'Quite right. She would have.'

'But that's impossible, isn't it? I mean, then, how is he also my twin?'

'The trouble with you humans is, you think time is a straight line. It isn't.'

That was it. The Seer turned to the assembled group and started telling a story about a beheading she had witnessed and two serpents that had emerged from it. Anya waited for a while, puzzled, but it was clear that that would be all Dhoomavati would say. She was rather full of tall tales that night.

The conversation was getting fuzzy. Parashuram asked Dhoomavati why she needed to smoke and drink so much. She replied that she was made that way; she was a goddess with insatiable hunger and thirst, and needs that could never be met; not that anyone else should try it. If they did they'd probably die. She added, by way of apology, 'The only reason

I'm not dead is because I can't. I have a horrible cough, though. Sometimes I cough out my intestines and have to stuff them back in.'

Prince Zohrab was talking of an exotic dancer he had known in the Chola empire who could still set his pulse racing. He got up to demonstrate to catcalls from the goddess and a disapproving look from Parashuram, at which point Anya and Bilal thought it best to walk away from the increasingly racy conversation.

They wandered down a narrow path, where it was relatively quieter.

'What are you thinking of, Anya?' asked Bilal.

'Feet,' she replied, quite truthfully. 'The prince's feet. And other things ...'

While she and Bilal had exchanged life stories already, she still did not want to voice her doubts to him.

'They're really rather funny, aren't they?' smiled Bilal. 'Those toes!'

'Exactly. I think I've seen them before somewhere. In a dream, or else ...'

'Why is it that our parents never told you about me?' asked Bilal. He was hurt by Anya's complete ignorance of his existence.

'Well, I suppose it's because your existence had

to be kept so secret that Ma felt compelled to hide it until the time was right,' reckoned Anya. 'Although, she sort of did refer—'

But Bilal was too impatient for this last bit. 'The time would never have been right if she hadn't been abducted, don't you think? And what about our father? Did he ever mention a son?'

Anya didn't have an answer. I wish they could do their own explaining, she thought.

'Do you think they're still alive?' Bilal asked, after a pause.

'I am sure Ma is,' said Anya, sticking her chin out. She didn't mention her father, not wanting to voice her fears. 'It seems like my dreams are real, so this has to be real, too. I just have to pay closer attention to them from now on. I need you to help me rescue her, Bilal. No one else seems to think it's that important. They're more concerned with saving the world, which is all very well, but she is the most important thing in the world for me. For me, she is the world.'

They walked silently for a few minutes.

'Do you think we can do it? Save the world, I mean,' Bilal asked, breaking the silence.

'What choice do we have? How can we let Kali's prisons multiply across the globe? We must at least try,' said Anya.

Rakshak met them at the end of the little path they had taken. 'Anya, would you mind letting me speak to your brother alone for a while? He'll join you at the camp in five minutes.'

'Go on, I expect he wants to thank you in private,' whispered Anya, nudging Bilal forward. Bilal took the left fork into the jungle with Rakshak, looking uncomfortable; he was not used to being thanked and dreaded what was coming.

Anya walked back, humming a tune—badly, as always. It seemed like ages since she'd felt this light-hearted. Yes, the road ahead would be tough, but tonight they were safe and she'd just found a brother who she had not known existed. That seemed enough for the moment.

Her mind went back to the prince's feet with their abnormally tall second toes. Where *have* I seen them before? It was no use. Her memory drew a blank. She was walking over a forest trail that was at a slightly higher altitude than the rest of the camp, when she felt, rather than heard, a distant roar.

Thunderstorm, I'd better get back.

The smoke screen above her tore apart into a million shreds. A livid red sky was raining enemy forces. By now, she knew the ringleaders: the demon with one hand and the terrible yellow eyes was at the north. He was huge, occupying half her sky as he materialised. To the southeast, a terrible woman, beautiful but with a cruel face, was fast forming. With a whoop of delight, she hacked away at a tree in front, making room for her men to land. Her forces fell on the ground like horrific raindrops, immediately doubling in number.

The west flank was headed by a balding soldier who had the largest forces under his command. From the height at which she stood Anya could see them cleaving through the jungle, clearing it with axes at every step. To her south was just one man: hollow cheekbones, deep set eyes, a walking skeleton. He came with a cloud of insects—what were they? Locusts, like in the Bible? Everything just wilted and died in their path as the man moved on relentlessly, looking neither right nor left as he headed towards the camp.

Anya hid behind a tree, watching them run straight towards the camp, desperately hoping they wouldn't change direction and find her.

She saw Dhoomavati flying straight up into the sky, a gigantic Karkash getting smaller in the distance. Anya heard the cries of Parashuram's army, clearly unprepared, as they got ready for battle. She saw Garud, flying up, then swooping down to attack the enemy troops, all the while checking out enemy positions. At least the prince was fighting. Then she heard Parashuram's yell and knew that one more wordkeeper was still alive. Garud's information must have worked.

Parashuram's soldiers avoided the north and the south and concentrated on the west flank, where the forces were mostly human, although the numbers were much larger.

Dhoomavati swooped towards the east, opening her mouth wide and swallowing everything in sight. The forces in the east got sucked up, as if by a giant vacuum cleaner. Their leader fought on, unfazed. Anya shuddered as she suddenly realised the goddess' terrible power. And she had thought this was a mad beggar woman!

This is far from over, thought Anya. They needed the combined forces of Rakshak and Bilal. In a trice, Anya went back the way she'd come, running as silently as she could until she came to the fork in the road, the left turn. She'd be all right with Rakshak by her side; Rakshak who'd taught her everything, was practically her guardian now, just like Bilal had his Parashuram.

She saw him in the distance, with his back to her, oddly calm. Hadn't he heard the din? Sheer relief overcame all the questions though. She ran up to Rakshak and hugged him. 'Thank god you're okay Rakshak! The enemy forces have attacked, again,

I'm so, so glad you're safe, we've got to go back now and join the fight—'

'Anya, don't!' Bilal's voice screeched at her from above. 'It's him, Anya, he's the secret weapon, he's been plotting this the whole time!'

Looking up, she saw Bilal trussed up against a branch, hanging upside down. The blood had already started rushing to his face.

Rakshak turned around to face her. A different Rakshak, far more handsome than before, but deadly cruel, with a cold smile that was enjoying every shred of her shock. Grabbing a handful of her short hair, he pulled Anya's head back as he yanked the chain with the four amulets off.

'Ah yes, not only the avatar, but the annoying sidekick as well, plus four amulets. Not a bad haul for my master. That would make nine amulets out of ten, you see. He already has five of them.'

He must mean Kali, thought Anya with the last vestiges of strength left in her. She slumped to the ground as he let her go. 'Why?' was all she managed to whisper.

'My dear, spoilt, twenty-first century brat, have you any idea what a five-thousand-year-long curse feels like?' Rakshak's lazy style of speech barely masked his long-suppressed rage. 'The unending pain, the oozing, the sores, the constant itching, the insults, the look of revulsion on everyone's face—do you think one can ever get used to it? And for what?'

'Mass murder, Ashwatthama,' said Anya, her fury lending an odd calm to her voice. 'You were cursed for mass murder.'

'I kept my word to Duryodhan, my friend, my king!' Rakshak was shouting now, a pulse throbbing in his temple. 'You think Arjun was any different? How many people did he kill? Since when did a war about property become a war of righteousness?'

'You killed sleeping people, when their defences were down. You murdered an unborn child, Ashwatthama. I know. I read it up.'

'And they deceived my father, their teacher and killed him! Arjun, his favourite, plotted his death! Yet they went unpunished! Try telling me that was right!' He took a deep breath and exhaled.

Anya didn't argue any further. Right and wrong seemed to be getting all muddled in her brain. Besides, she was sinking rapidly.

'Every day of my interminable life, I plotted revenge on Krishna. He would not be a god forever. He would be human again, and then, then I would take my revenge. And so, I waited.

'I did go to the Red Planet, Anya—or Vishasha, as it is now called. What I didn't tell you is that I met Kali there. A much weakened, exiled Kali, but still keen on returning victorious. We had an enemy in common—you know what they say about your enemy's enemy ... and why not? Krishna's human life would be over in a blink. The changes he had brought about were purely cosmetic, nothing had altered the greed in the hearts of humankind, so the time would be ripe just afterwards.

'I became Kali's secret weapon. I was to go back, befriend the wordkeepers, keep an eye on successive generations and try to track Balram. As Krishna had said, Balram would find Kalki—for me.'

Anya strained her ears. The battle sounds seemed to be receding. Something had happened. She gave Rakshak her full attention, hoping he would not realise that the tide may have turned.

'Funny, Krishna never did account for Balram's eternal gullibility. Once your mother was taken, it was child's play to invade your dreams and lure you to me. You see, the Chiranjeevi mentioned in the letter wasn't me, but the prince. I was just the guide appointed at Asirgarh, the guardian who would take you to him. You must have realised that Zohrab wasn't born yesterday. Prince Zohrab—or Vibhishan—is the actual wordkeeper meant to look after you. He's clever, our prince. Realised the danger you were in and attempted to contact you beforehand on the train. I had to organise a mock attack just to make sure you met me first, so I could find out all you knew and then mould you as I wanted.'

With a flash, Anya remembered why she felt she had seen the prince's feet before. They belonged to the sleeping passenger in her compartment on the train. Her head was spinning very hard now; the searing pain from her wound was spreading to other parts of her body like wildfire. The poison must be travelling through my bloodstream, she thought. All for nothing. It was all such a waste. Her breath grew shallow.

She felt, rather than saw, Dhoomavati's crazy face, motioning her to keep quiet. Keep him talking, Anya. Distract him, she thought.

'So you sent the yaksha?'

'He was bound to me by a debt and had to do as I asked. Strangely enough, he seemed rather reluctant to abduct you. I never could figure out the reason. I know he keeps an unnaturally close watch on you, though—I've felt his presence. Why?' Rakshak leaned over and jerked her head up by the hair.

Anya suddenly knew what those barely heard whispers were. It was the yaksha warning her against Rakshak. Except, for some reason he could not name Ashwatthama.

The sounds around her had been fading, but now

it all went silent. She let out the lightest of breaths. She felt nothingness, but no calm. Is this death?

A sudden yell jolted her awake. Bilal had jumped off the tree, free of his bonds, a small knife in his hand. At the same instant, Karkash and Dhoomavati swooped in, the crow's huge wings partially blocking Anya's vision.

Bilal leapt on Ashwatthama, piercing his heart with the knife right up to the hilt, and Karkash pecked clean through a lung. Rakshak fell back on the ground with a mighty thud, his dying face full of surprise.

Yanking the stones off Rakshak's body, Bilal placed them on Anya's lifeless chest.

'Breathe, Anya, breathe,' said Dhoomavati, rubbing the girl's palms vigorously.

Warmth was returning. Anya could hear voices in the distance. Feebly opening her eyes, she saw Dhoomavati first. The goddess was threading the amulets through a strand of her own hair, careful to let the stones touch Anya's skin all the while.

'I didn't die,' she managed to say.

'No, no you didn't,' Bilal was alternately crying and smiling.

'Although she's far from well, Kalki—so don't excite her,' warned Dhoomavati. She spoke in the calmest voice she could muster. 'Parashuram and the prince are alive, and they've been able to beat back the forces for the night. We'll have to move to another camp immediately, of course. The Enemy got to know of this one through Ashwatthama, he was informing them all the while.'

Rakshak's body lay in the distance—his eyes wide open and surprised.

'How can he be dead? I thought he was immortal,' whispered Anya.

'I think he became mortal from the moment the curse lifted,' explained Dhoomavati. 'He wasn't expecting that, though. You can see the surprise on his face.'

'What shall we do now, Bilal?'

'We shall focus on you getting better first.'

'But …'

'Hush,' he said, shutting her eyes with his palm.

And so, Anya slept.

RAKSHAS TAL

A month had passed since the ambush. Their army had been reduced to a rag-tag bunch of survivors and the wordkeepers. Desperate to save themselves, they had asked Karkash to fly them to a secret location that only Parashuram knew of.

The bird had flown them far north, crossing the Indian and the Nepalese borders into Tibet. There, they found themselves in a monastery carved out of the rock face. There were no spires and no flags visible from the outside. It was as if it was meant to be hidden away forever.

'Welcome to Shambhal,' said Parashuram. Anya and the rest of the group were directed to one of the outcrops that was hollowed out and camouflaged to create quarters for the monks. Each room consisted of two narrow beds, rugs and felt for warmth and a box for storage of bare essentials. It was a spartan arrangement, but compared to the inhospitable climate outside, they were in the lap of luxury.

The monks had a different name for the place. They called it Shangri-La.

Inhospitable it might have been, but the surroundings were breathtakingly beautiful. The brown of the rocks and the pristine white of the snow formed striking patterns across the landscape. The air was thin but unbelievably pure. At night, the whole place gleamed blue in the reflected moonlight, its beauty hushing every visitor into silence. Out here, the primacy of nature was assured—both in its beauty and its ruthlessness.

Anya healed well in the monastery. She had spent the first few nights in delirium and high fever, but then the amazing curative properties of Shambhal percolated down to her being and she found herself recovering fast. Thanks to the able ministrations of Dhoomavati and plenty of rest, she could now move about, although combat was still out of the question.

Bilal was her constant companion through all of this. The two were inseparable, as if they wanted to make up for their years apart. They often took long walks, discussing the events of their recent past.

On this day, the two of them had left for a hike at dawn at Dhoomavati's suggestion. The morning dew here, she said, would help in Anya's recovery and they were instructed to stay outdoors for the entire day. The children were provided with bags of food and dried fruits to sustain themselves.

Dressed in the garb of young lamas as a precaution, Anya and Bilal set out. They walked on for a good five miles, their bags slung over their shoulders, until they reached the base of the mountains.

An enormous crescent-shaped lake lay in front of them. They could not see the other side. It seemed like the world had ended here, into this limitless body of water as it merged with the blue sky ahead.

'I don't understand how Rakshak could be such an ardent devotee of Shiva and so vindictive at the same time. Didn't he see the harm he was causing?' said Anya, still fretting about what had happened.

'He was always like that, Anya. He had such potential for greatness, but he could not look beyond his slighted ego and his seething rage. It consumed him five thousand years ago, and he let his resentment fester for this long.'

The lake loomed large in front of them, still, huge and forbidding. Its dark blue depths seemed to draw Anya closer as she stared at it.

'Funny how some people never learn. Where are we, Bilal? Is this Mansarovar?'

'No, this is Rakshas Tal, its dark twin. The water of this lake is salty and doesn't sustain any life. That's why it's so eerie and still. Mansarovar is further beyond.'

Rakshas Tal—the lake of the rakshasas—Anya mulled over the name. 'What are those islands in the middle?'

'Rakshas Tal has four islands. They're inaccessible in the summer, but it's possible to visit them once the lake freezes over. I came here once while you were ill.'

They walked through the outcrop of rock till they were close to the edge of the lake.

A giant stone statue stood beside it—the face of a man, the body of a bird.

Anya stared at the statue in disbelief—its face was oddly familiar. 'Why, it's ...'

'Greetings, wordkeeper,' said the statue as it moved to greet her, making her jump.

The yaksha.

'You rescued me in the train,' said Anya.

'And warned you—at the station, in the jungle the other day—but I was bound by a promise through Ashwatthama's lifetime and couldn't tell you anything specific about the secret weapon.'

Anya realised how familiar the yaksha's voice sounded.

'Tell me, if Rakshak was all bad, why did he tell me how to find Kali's abode and my mother?'

'You and Kalki were being thrown a bait, Anya. A really tempting one, too. They wanted to capture the two of you as you entered Vishasha through the portal. It's probably why your mother is still alive.'

Anya spun around towards Bilal, an edge of desperation to her voice. 'You're not thinking of backing out, Bilal? Not now? This is the only way our family can be together again!'

'Of course not. Besides, you need the other six amulets. But we need another route in, a different one from the one Rakshak talked about. Remember, they'll be watching that one like a hawk.'

'Which is where Rakshas Tal comes in,' said the yaksha. 'Mansarovar is known as a lake of great power, where the gods are very near to humans. But Rakshas Tal is far more important to us right now. Legend has it that Ravan himself worshipped Shiva here for his supernatural powers. What does Kali want above all else?' The yaksha looked as if he expected an answer.

'Divinity. He wants to be worshipped instead of Shiva and Vishnu. In temples, in homes, officially, not just covertly,' said Bilal.

'Yes, he is obsessed with all the symbolism associated with Shiva and Vishnu. He covets their temples, their idols, their paintings, their devotees, their ...'

'Lake,' finished Anya for him. Everyone knew of the connection between the gods and Mansarovar. 'So he wants to conquer Mansarovar?'

'Not quite. Ask yourself this, if you were Kali, where would you have your abode?'

'Well, Kailash is supposed to be Shiva's abode and its straight ahead from Mansarovar, so ...'

'I've got it,' said a triumphant Bilal. 'He wants a marker to his abode like Mansarovar is a marker to Kailash, except the lake in question is Rakshas Tal.'

'So we look ahead from Rakshas Tal in the same way,' finished Anya.

The yaksha picked up the children in his claws and flew high up in the air. Used to the comfortable whoosh-whoosh of wings at their ears by now, they concentrated on searching for the portal.

Beneath them lay the circular, lighter water body that was Mansarovar and the darker crescent that was Rakshas Tal curved to its left. Ahead, Mount Kailash gleamed like a faceted crystal, its stepped rocks coated with ice. There was nothing on earth to match it: no other focal point quite as riveting. The children gasped at the beauty. The yaksha, who had seen it many times before, was unmoved. He simply flew on a little further and said: 'There.'

The air in front of them was really thin—even the atmosphere looked translucent, as if one could just push one's hand through. Gingerly, Anya did just that. Her hand disappeared into the mist up to the wrist. Carefully, she pulled it back. The air in front seemed to stitch itself together in an instant. On her hand was a light layer of red dust.

They were too amazed to speak; instead they stared at the red dust, not daring to push their hands in a second time, but certain now in their knowledge of a new world just next to theirs.

'That is the official entrance to Vishasha and it is always guarded. To get past, you will have to be unseen. Bilal can vanish, but Anya, that's impossible for you,' said the yaksha after they landed on solid ground.

'I'm not staying behind,' she said immediately, sticking out her chin.

The yaksha nodded, then continued, 'I'm coming to that. Yakshas can be invisible twice a day, along with any thing or anyone on their person at those times.'

'What are these times?' asked Anya.

'Dawn and dusk,' said the yaksha. 'So we wait.'

They sat near the lake as the afternoon wore on, discussing future plans.

'You do realise that once we're in, we're on our own and can be discovered any time,' warned Bilal.

Anya nodded. She knew the risks.

Finally, sunset arrived. The sun turned a glowing red and gradually lowered itself beyond the horizon. A magical hour was approaching: everything was lit in a grey light, but the moon was not yet up, night hadn't fallen.

Beside them, the yaksha shimmered. 'Quick, get on my back!' he commanded. The children climbed on, holding on to the yaksha's back, watching their own palms shimmer and then turn transparent. They could see the lakes gleaming through their skin. They flew off, straight above Rakshas Tal and ahead.

The sky seemed to turn a misty grey; they flew right through and straight ahead into a red world with its red moons, leaving their own familiar Earth and its blue-green beauty ruthlessly behind.

EPILOGUE

At Port Blair, on a deserted rooftop, sat a strange object: it was a large, eye-shaped thing, with a green iris and sandy lashes. The eye was staring at a little red patch in the sky that would appear and disappear every fortnight.

The locals had expected an advertisement or a billboard to follow this strange installation, but nothing else had been added and bit by bit, it lost its novelty. People went about their daily business, scarcely noticing it any more or what it was staring at.

The eye sat motionless on the rooftop as it was directed to do: *some day, they would come.*

Acknowledgements

Huge thanks to Amish Tripathi, Anirban Sen, Aniruddha Sen, Anish Sarkar, Bharath Patil, Dipali Chakraborti, Dharmendra Gaddam, Harsho Mohan Chattoraj, Indira Basu, Jai Zende, Madhubani Sengupta and Sanjay Gupta for your invaluable help, comments and encouragement.

A big thank you to my parents for their complete faith in me through this process.

A salute to one of my idols, Satyajit Ray, for the idea of the large second toes on a sleeping man as a clue. I loved it so much since childhood that I felt compelled to put it in my debut novel.

Most people count themselves lucky if they have one good editor—I had two brilliant ones. Thanks for everything, Sayoni Basu and Anushka Ravishankar.

To Ayan Sen: in all things I love, I find you.

JASH SEN is a DU, IIM graduate who worked in IT and taught mathematics while dreaming of writing a book. *The Wordkeepers* is Jash's first novel, and is the first of a trilogy.

Jash likes bourbon biscuits, bookstores, libraries, reading, well-stuffed armchairs, watching films (especially thrillers) and spinning stories.

www.wordkeepers.com
www.facebook.com/Jash Sen
authorjashsen@gmail.com